Betrayed

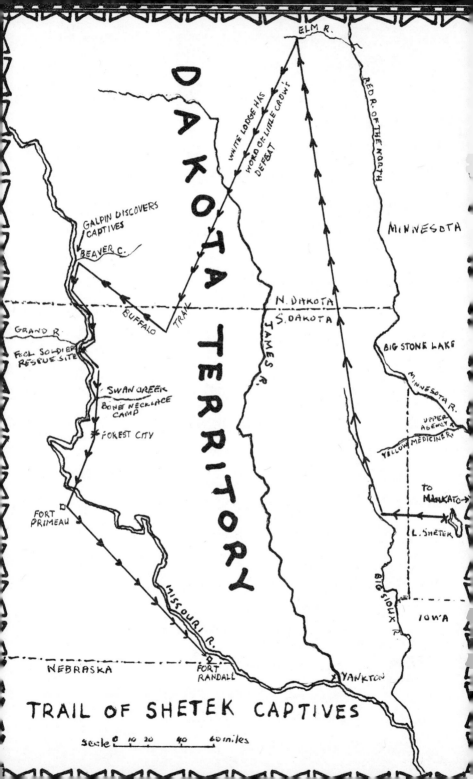

TRAIL OF SHETEK CAPTIVES

Scale 0 10 20 40 60 miles

Betrayed

by Virginia Driving Hawk Sneve

HOLIDAY HOUSE
New York

Frontispiece map and ornaments
by Chief Oren Lyons

LIBRARY OF CONGRESS CATALOGING IN PUBLICATION DATA
Sneve, Virginia Driving Hawk.
Betrayed.
SUMMARY: Relates the events of the Santee Indian
raid on the Lake Shetek, Minnesota, settlement and the
subsequent fate of the captives.
1. Dakota Indians—Wars, 1862-1865—Juvenile fiction.
[1. Dakota Indians—Wars, 1862-1865—Fiction. 2. Indians of North America—Captivities—Fiction] I. Title.
PZ7.S679Be   [Fic]   74-7574
ISBN 0-8234-0243-6

For Mother

Contents

AUTHOR'S NOTE

The author has retained the true names of the characters and places and followed as closely as possible the actual historic evidence for the incidents of this episode, which occurred in 1862. However, the author was not confined by bare historic facts and used her imagination to develop characters, dialogue, and situations.

VIRGINIA DRIVING HAWK SNEVE

Betrayed

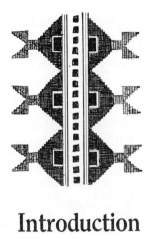

Introduction

In the beginning months of 1862 the Sioux, or Dakota Indians, lived quietly within the boundaries set aside for them by the United States Government. In Minnesota the Santee Sioux had been learning to farm their lands around the Lower Agency on the Minnesota River, the Upper Agency, three miles from the Yellow Medicine River, and at Big Stone Lake which bordered Minnesota and what is now South Dakota.

The Yankton Sioux lived quietly on their reservation in Dakota Territory on the Missouri River. The untamed Yanktonais Sioux ranged freely in their lands between Big Stone Lake and the Missouri River.

The Teton Sioux were peaceful in their territory that began on the western shore of the Missouri River, and they still hunted as far as the Big Horn Mountains.

All was calm in Sioux country, and the United States was fully occupied with its Civil War. Therefore, on August 18, 1862, great shock reverberated in the East with the news that the passive Santee, who had been exposed to Christianity and civilization longer than the other Sioux tribes, had started a ruthless war. They scoured the upper Minnesota River Valley of some seven hundred settlers and one hundred soldiers. Those whites who were not killed, mainly women and children, were taken into captivity. The survivors told tales of horrible butchery.

The good citizens of the United States were alarmed and appalled by the atrocities committed by the Santee. Some believed that the uprising had been incited by Confederates from the South. Others insisted that the Indians were naturally treacherous and all should have been killed instead of given good farm land. These good people never looked to themselves for a reason for the brief but brutal battle. They did not know that Santee hearts had been in a ferment of dissatisfaction for many years before 1862.

White treachery had been blatantly involved in the

signing of the 1851 Traverse des Sioux Treaty under which the Santee were guaranteed $200,000 by the United States Government for the sale of their lands. After the chiefs signed the Traverse des Sioux paper at one table they were quickly ushered to a second table where they were told to put their marks on another paper. The Santee leaders, ignorant of the white man's mode of contract, believed they were signing two copies of one treaty. Instead, they unwittingly agreed to the terms of the "traders' paper," which allowed the governor of Minnesota Territory, Alexander Ramsey, to turn the money over to the traders, who would first deduct the tribes' debts. Knowing that the Santee were coming into money, the traders had liberally extended credit to the Indians; they then multiplied these debts and even demanded payment for debtors who were dead.

The Santee angrily filed a protest with Governor Ramsey who listened and assured the Indians that the money would be paid according to the treaty. But Ramsey had already disbursed some of the money to the traders and would not give any to the Santee until they signed a receipt showing that they had received the full amount. Without their annuities, the Santee were soon at the point of starvation.

After the new Republican administration came into

office in 1861, Clark W. Thompson, newly appointed superintendent for the Minnesota area, visited the Upper and Lower Agencies in July, 1861, to supervise the annuity payments. He listened to the grievances of the Indians and to their reports of the many wrongs they had suffered. Although Thompson was inexperienced in dealing with Indians, he had humanitarian feelings for the red men in his care. He promised the Santee that all of the wrongs of the past would be righted and further promised them another payment in the fall. The Santee believed Thompson and instead of harvesting their crops and going on the fall hunt to prepare for winter, they all came to the agencies to await the promised bounty. When it came, it amounted to only two dollars and fifty cents per head. The Santee were destitute, and the agencies had many hungry Indians to feed that winter.

Beyond the treachery of the Traverse des Sioux Treaty and an unfulfilled promise, the Santee had been hearing that the United States Army was weak and doing poorly in its war with the South. The Indians had not only lost faith in the word of the United States, but now they had no respect or fear for its armed strength. To the Santee, the time was right to rise up in desperate anger against the only representatives of the United States that they knew— the white settlers of the Minnesota Valley.

The main body of the Santee attacked Fort Ridgely and New Ulm. Smaller raids were made in southwestern Minnesota, and it is one of these that is the basis for this story.

I

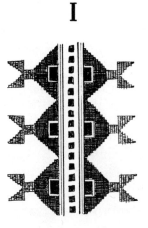

Waanatan, The Charger

"*Hiyohi!*" commanded the *Eyapaha* as he wound his way through the village. "Come, people of the Two Kettles, the bravest and strongest of the Teton! Gather to hear of our cousins the Santee. Their chief, Taoya Te Duta, who is also called Little Crow, has sent his emissary to tell us of the war in the Minnesota land. *Upo!*"

Waanatan, The Charger, and his brother-friend, Kills And Comes, looked up from their task of stripping bark from slender branches as they heard the summons of the camp crier. The young men watched the *Eyapaha* as he walked on repeating his message. They wanted to join the villagers already moving toward the camp's center but dared not leave their work until their teacher, Itazipe, the bow maker, gave his permission.

Itazipe gave no sign that he heard the summons, for he was intent in tying the rawhide string of a new bow and he would not be interrupted until it was securely bound. Many warriors and hunters of the Two Kettle tribe depended on the old man for well-made weapons, and he would not hurry his work. Finally, Itazipe tied the last knot, examined the bow, and gave a satisfied grunt. He carried the bow into his lodge and then signaled to Charger and Kills And Comes that they might leave.

Eagerly, the two young men moved to where the Council sat surrounded by the villagers. They were excited by the *Eyapaha's* summons. For weeks, in the Moon When All Things Ripen, there had been rumors of the Santee uprising against the whites, and the Teton longed for first-hand knowledge. Some of the young men, eager for the glory of battle long denied them in treaty lands, had volunteered to go east for news. But their elders forbade any action which could be interpreted by the white soldiers as giving aid to the Santee. "Wait," the old men counseled. "Wait. Word will come."

Now the emissary of Little Crow had arrived in the Two Kettle village, which spread in the traditional horn shape above the place called Fort Pierre on the west side of the *Minnishoshay*, the Missouri River. The lean and wiry Santee warrior standing in the center of the Council displayed his tribe's contact with the whites by the U. S. Army issue shirt and shapeless trousers he wore. His hair was held back by a ragged cotton band from which a single feather hung. His moccasins were worn thin and his face was gaunt, but his eyes burned fiercely in their sunken sockets. It was evident that he had traveled far and fast seeking Teton bands.

The Santee was speaking as Charger and Kills And Comes neared the edge of the crowd, and they could hear the "d" sound of the man's speech. The young men smiled at each other. To their ears the unfamiliar dialect was harsh and amusing with its lack of the rhythmic "l" of the Teton. But they understood every word and they pushed forward the better to see and hear, even though they were too young and inexperienced to have an active voice in the Council.

"Taoya Te Duta, who also bears the name of Little Crow, sends his greetings," the Santee said. "His heart is filled with love and great respect for his cousins, the brave and strong Teton. Alas," the Santee hung his head sadly, "Little Crow's heart is also filled with sadness for our people who have been starving. The annuities promised to us have not come, and the many whites in our land have driven away the game. Our children cry with pain of hunger in their bellies."

The mothers among the Two Kettle pulled their blankets over their faces and cried aloud with sympathy, for none of the Sioux—Santee or Teton— ever willingly let their children go hungry. The Santee stood with his head lowered and waited until the women's wails were stilled and then he shouted, "But worse is the treachery shown us by the white fathers! They promised food, clothing, and money when we signed the paper that said we gave up our lands. They lied!" he growled. "There is no food. Our clothing is ragged. There is no money to buy provisions."

He glared at the Two Kettles and then went on, softly, "We are told that our annuities have been de- layed because the whites fight among themselves. We are told that the soldiers of the whites are weak and are losing their war. Why," his voice rose again, "should the Santee suffer so that the whites can win their war?" He stared about him.

"We are a desperate people," the Santee continued, "but we still retain the pride of the Sioux. We will not let ourselves be treated worse than dogs in a time of famine. We fight! We kill the treacherous whites who took our land with only lies in payment! We burn the homes of the settlers who have spread like lice on our land. We are at war!"

Many of the young men around Charger and Kills And Comes were moved by the Santee's eloquence. They shook their fists in the air as if brandishing weapons, and war cries were heard; but the Council was silent.

"Taoya Te Duta sends greetings to his Teton cousins, and invites you to join the Santee in a great war against the whites! Join us!" the warrior cried, looking over the heads of the old men to the young men who yearned for war. "Together we will drive the whites from the land of the Sioux forever!"

Now there was a mighty roar of approval from the young men and also from the older accomplished warriors who had chafed at their long inactivity. Then One Feather, an old wise man of the Council, spoke and his voice carried through the tumult, "We have heard that in this war the Santee have killed white women and murdered their children."

Silence fell upon the crowd as the elder spoke, for although the Teton were fierce in battle, they fought only men.

The Santee warrior drew himself up so that he appeared as tall as his Teton cousins, and there was no doubt among the Two Kettles that he was a proud man. "True," he answered the charge without shame. And before the people could express their disapproval, he hurried on, "White squaws breed faster than good Dakota women. Their children grow to breed more. Shakopee, a great Santee, has said that the white men are like the locusts that fly so thickly that the sky is as a snow storm. Kill one, two, ten or even as many as the leaves in the forest, but they will not be missed." The warrior looked among the now-quiet Two Kettles and shouted, "There are too many whites in our land now!" He held the people in silence with his fierce gaze.

"The Santee," he spoke in a soft sad voice, "have known the whites far longer than our cousins. Count on your fingers all the day long and the whites will come faster than you can count. They have pushed us out of our lake lands into the little space of the Minnesota Valley. As they have moved into our country, we have learned too well that the whites show no mercy for our women and children. You will see," his voice rose in warning, "someday the whites will covet this land of yours, and then you will learn of their treachery."

Murmurs of disbelief went among the Two Kettles, for they and all the Teton tribes were strong and feared by the whites.

Another old man spoke. "We have heard that if the white women and children are not killed, the Santee take them as captives and slaves."

"Have the Teton never taken captives?" the Santee warrior retorted. But his scorn was ignored as the same old man spoke again, "We have also heard that these captives go naked, are starved and beaten, and that they will all be killed in time."

"We are a poor people!" the warrior cried desperately, realizing that he was losing what little support he had among the Two Kettles. "Would you have us take food from the mouths of our children or leave them naked so that white children can be fat and warm?"

There was a great hubbub among the Two Kettles as some expressed sorrow over the plight of white captives and others agreed with the Santee. Charger felt sadness as he thought about children made into slaves and he shouted, "You are doing a bad thing!" But the Santee did not hear him and no one else listened. Although Charger was in his nineteenth winter, he was not considered a man yet and his voice was not heeded.

"The buffalo herds are going fast even from our country," spoke a Two Kettle man who was a hunter. "We know that the Santee have been ranging into our land to kill our game. We cannot be allies of a people who steal from their cousins."

Many Two Kettle voices called out "*Ho,*" and "*Han,*" in agreement.

"That is true," spoke another who was skilled as a trapper. "And consider this; if we go to war with the whites, the traders will leave us. They will take with them the coffee and sugar, the flour, the blankets, ammunition for our guns, and many other things for which we trade our furs."

There was much talk among the people now as they considered the reasons for not going to the aid of the Santee. They argued or agreed among themselves even as the Council retired to the chief's lodge to debate the Santee's request more thoroughly. Little Crow's emissary stood downcast and alone in the midst of the babbling Teton.

Charger and Kills And Comes walked away from the excited talk of the young men who longed for war. The two friends also wanted to know the glories of battle, but not with the Santee.

Both of the young men, close in age, were tall and slim. Charger's skin was a shade lighter than that of

Kills And Comes, his hair more brown than the blue-black of the Two Kettles. Charger had long been known to have sympathy for the white man. He spoke with the traders, trappers, and soldiers who traveled the *Minnishoshay* and had learned English well so that he was often called to act as an interpreter.

The Two Kettles said that Charger's understanding of the whites and English came easily to the young man because he had the blood of that race in his veins. It was well known among the village that Charger's grandfather was the explorer, Meriwether Lewis. Many of the old men of the tribe remembered the 1804 visit of Lewis and Clark, and Charger was proud of his ancestry.

Charger and Kills And Comes spoke quietly together. "The Santee spoke falsely of the white men," Charger said. "The whites cannot all be the way he said."

"True," Kills And Comes agreed and would have said more, but now the Council emerged from their meeting lodge and a shout went up from the people. The *Eyapaha* began his rounds even as the crowd dispersed and called out that the Two Kettles would remain neutral and let the Santee fight their own war.

"*Ho, waste*, good!" shouted Charger along with many of the people. He felt a burning in his soul and added slowly, as if in a daze, "It is a bad thing the Santee have done. Bad to make captives of white women and children," he went on, hearing his words coming without his will, and he turned in confusion to Kills And Comes. "I—I," Charger stammered, trying to control his rushing thoughts, "I—will—will rescue them."

The crowd was still after his vow and then there was laughter and derisive hoots from some who had not seen Charger's strained face as he had spoken.

"How will you find the captives?" someone shouted.

"The Santee will kill you," cried another, "for they will be angry that the Two Kettles will not help them."

But Kills And Comes shouted, "Be still!" He held his arm about Charger's shoulders in support as his friend seemed near to fainting. "My brother-friend's words are not of his own will. See," Kills And Comes cried to those around, "he is in a trance!"

Now there were murmurs of confusion and awe from the Two Kettle who realized that Charger had been touched by *Wakantanka*.

One of the old men of the Council was standing near and saw and heard Charger's strange, uncontrolled speech. He came up to the young men and spoke softly to Kills And Comes, "Is this youth your brother-friend?"

"*Han*, yes," answered Kills And Comes, "we have been so since childhood."

"Have you both made your vision quest?"

"*Hiya*, no," Kills And Comes shook his head. "We have not had a sign to tell us it is time."

"Until now," said the old man.

"*Ho*," agreed Kills And Comes, "my brother-friend has now been struck by *Wakantanka*, but I have not."

"Did you not know before any other that Charger's words were not of his own will?"

Kills And Comes humbly hung his head, but he still retained his hold on Charger who heard and saw nothing.

"Go to your teacher, Itazipe," ordered the old man for he knew that the boys' fathers and grandfathers were dead. "He will instruct you."

Kills And Comes led Charger, who meekly followed, to the bow maker's tipi. The news of Charger's *wakan* experience had preceded the young men and Itazipe was waiting for them.

Charger came to himself as Kills And Comes helped him to sit. His face became wet with sweat and he looked about in confusion.

"Do not speak," warned Itazipe. "Empty your minds of thought as I prepare you for your quest."

Itazipe took a sacred red pipe from a bag and stood before the young men. He picked up a live coal from the tipi's center fire and lit the pipe. Before he drew smoke into his lungs he offered the pipe to the North, the East, the West, the South, up to Father Sky, down to Mother Earth, and last to the center of his being. "Do this," Itazipe instructed, "and the smallness of man will merge into the greatness of all."

He handed the pipe to the young men and watched as each made his offering with the pipe. When they were finished, he took the pipe and placed it before him as he sat and spoke.

"My sons, *Wakantanka* has touched you. He wishes you to go to a high place where you will take no food and no water for four days and nights or until He sends a vision to you. It may be that one of you will have his sacred dream before the other. If that is so, then the first to dream must not disturb his brother, but leave him until the end of four days and nights.

"It may also be," Itazipe continued, "that only one of you will have the vision. If this be so, then the medicine of the vision belongs to both." He sat quietly for a time as the young men watched their teacher's every move.

"My sons," Itazipe began again, "when you reach the high place remove all thoughts from your minds. Then think only of *Wakantanka* and of His strength, mystery, and beauty. Pray to Him to help you and to help your people. Make yourself one with Him so that your prayers will rise like the Thunder Bird to the sky. Humble yourselves so that your whole body becomes your ears and eyes that you may receive and accept what *Wakantanka* sends."

Itazipe rose and signaled for Charger and Kills And Comes to follow. They walked through the village where the women were busy preparing the evening meal and the men sat talking about the days events. None spoke to Itazipe or to the young men. No one wished to disturb thoughts filled with new *wakan* instructions.

Itazipe led Charger and Kills And Comes to a sandy spit on the river where Charger saw that his mother and the mother of Kills And Comes had built a sweat hut of willow branches covered with skins. The women were tending a roaring fire near the entrance. When the boys' mothers saw the men approaching, they left without speaking. Waiting nearby was Swift Bear, a young man of Charger's own age, who had already made a successful vision quest. Itazipe spoke to Swift Bear.

"Are you willing to accompany these friends on their quest?"

Swift Bear nodded.

"Will you encourage them if they falter? Assist

them with the pipe if their memory fails? Pray for them and with them?"

To each of Itazipe's questions Swift Bear nodded.

"*Ho, waste*," Itazipe said, and led Charger and Kills And Comes into the sweat hut.

They removed their garments, headbands, and moccasins. Itazipe gave each a drink of clear water and left them. Soon he returned carrying a red hot stone from the fire in two smoking branches. Swift Bear followed with another stone. Twice this was done. Then Itazipe entered with a bladder skin filled with water. He poured it over the stones, and thick, heavy steam filled the hut. The boys did not see when Itazipe fastened the opening tightly so that none of the cool evening air could enter nor the smothering steam escape.

Twice more Itazipe and Swift Bear carried hot stones within and poured water over them. At last, when Charger and Kills And Comes were near fainting and could bear no more, Itazipe ripped away the covering of the hut. He jerked Charger to his feet and Swift Bear pulled up Kills And Comes. The perspiring, naked youths ran to the river and plunged in.

Shock! Shock! Charger thought he was dying, yet from his mouth a song burst and Kills And Comes joined in the mysterious chant of praise to *Wakan-tanka* for their purification.

When the brother-friends left the river and dressed in clean garments brought by their mothers, Swift Bear led them to where the women had tethered three bridled horses. No word of farewell was spoken. The three young men mounted and rode off to the west where stand the high buttes.

II

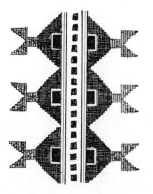

Slaughter Slough

Sarah Duley awoke to hear her mother humming a happy song. The girl smelled coffee boiling and the delicious scent of biscuits baking for breakfast. Sarah stretched under the covers but was careful not to distrub her younger sister, Nancy, who was sleeping beside her. She peered through the rip in the blanket that was hung on a line to set aside the girls' sleeping place in the main room of the cabin.

Sarah watched her mother move the boiling pot to the back of the polished cast iron stove and gave a little sigh of sympathy for her. Martha Duley was a slender woman of average height whose face, unsoftened by faded blond hair pulled into a tight bun, showed the strain of the hard life of a settler's wife. She looked older than her thirty-two years. The woman turned from the stove and Sarah saw the content look on her mother's face and was glad that at last the Duleys were in their own home. Her mother had been so unhappy in the large communal cabin built and shared by the Duley, Wright, and Ireland families who came from Wisconsin to the Lake Shetek settlement in 1858. The log structure had been crowded and the petty bickering of the women and the childrens' constant turmoil had distressed Martha Duley more than anyone else. Again Sarah sighed as she remembered how frightened she had been when her mother became strangely quiet and moved as if she didn't know or care where she was. Now, thank goodness, her mother was all right. The Duleys and the Irelands had built cabins last year and the Wrights had stayed in the first building. Five other families from Wisconsin and Ohio also came to farm the rich soil around the lake and slough, and erected individual cabins. Once Martha Duley was alone and secure with only the members of her family to contend with, she had regained her cheerful sweet nature.

"Sarah, Nancy." The girl's half-awake thoughts were interrupted by her mother's call. "Time to get up, girls. Sarah, help Nancy do her hair."

"Yes, Mama," Sarah answered and nudged nine-year-old Nancy who mumbled and burrowed deeper into her pillow. Sarah shook her sister harder and wondered what it would be like to be a younger child rather than the eldest who had to do so much work. Her pa, William, was always saying, "Sarah, you're the oldest—going to be thirteen—a young lady. You're too old to be spending your time in play. Help your mother with her chores and watch over the young ones so they don't get into mischief or hurt themselves."

A little angry now, Sarah jerked the reluctant Nancy awake. The little girl whined, "Mama, Sarah hurt me."

"Shush," Sarah hissed as she began to dress, "I didn't hurt you. You're just too hard to rouse. Now, get up so that I can braid your hair after I do mine."

As Sarah pulled the blanket aside and walked to the washstand by the door, her mother climbed up the ladder to the loft where her two little brothers slept. "Wake up, boys," her mother called. "Billy," she said to the ten-year old, "rouse Robert. Help him button his britches."

Sarah gave a satisfied smile. At least she didn't have to dress the wiggly little Robert any more. That was Billy's task now and he was welcome to it.

"Hurry now," Martha urged as she backed down

the ladder. "Your pa will be in from chores soon."

" 'Morning, Mama," Sarah said and smiled with her mother as they listened to the thumps and squeals of the boys from above.

" 'Morning, Sarah," Martha answered. "Is Nancy up?"

In answer Nancy came into the main room of the cabin and made a rush for the door. "I'm going to help Pa carry in the milk," she announced.

"Just you wait, young lady," Martha said, grabbing the little girl's arm. "You set yourself down and let Sarah do your hair."

"Aw," Nancy complained, "can't I leave yesterday's braids in today? Sarah hurts too much when she combs my hair."

"Well," Sarah scolded, "if you'd sit still and not jerk around it wouldn't hurt so much!"

Mrs. Duley playfully tugged the little girl's braids and then gave her youngest daughter a hug as the child gave an outraged yelp.

The boys came shouting and tumbling down the loft ladder when, over their happy noise, Sarah heard a gunshot. She looked at her mother; Martha had heard it, too. Then, through the open door, they saw William Duley running to the house.

"Indians!" he shouted as he came into the cabin.

"Quick!" he urged Martha, who stood rooted in terror. He gave her a gentle push and herded the children toward the door. "They're at the Irelands now. We've got to get to the big cabin so we can make a stand. Hurry!" he commanded, "I'll follow you with the gun."

Martha gave a despairing look at her beloved cabin, grabbed up the youngest, four-year old Robert, and ran. Sarah took Nancy's hand; Billy followed, and they fled for their lives.

Outside, Sarah saw smoke rising from the Ireland cabin a mile away. The Irelands, too, were running to the big communal cabin which stood on the edge of the Duley land near the slough. Nancy stumbled; as Sarah stopped to help her up she glanced back and saw Indians enter her home. Her father turned to fire at the savages, but they were too busy looting the cabin to pursue.

As his family hurried into the large cabin, Thomas Ireland dropped to one knee to cover the fleeing Duleys. Sarah heard Indian whoops and chilling yells as she followed her mother and brothers to safety. Her father came close behind, and as soon as he reached the cabin Ireland leaped inside and dropped the stout wooden bar into place to bolt the door.

There were thirty-four people crowded together in

the Wrights' large cabin, which had been the communal lodge. The eleven men dislodged the chinking from between the logs and fired their rifles through the gaps at the Indians who were leaping and yelling just out of range. The eight women and their fifteen children huddled together in the center of the room. Nancy and Sarah clung to each other near their mother, who was holding the boys. "They've fired your house, Duley!" shouted a settler who was watching out of the window. Martha fainted.

"Mama, Mama," Sarah called, pushing her brothers away from the unconscious woman. She began chafing her mother's wrists.

One of the women brought water and a cloth, and Sarah applied a compress to her mother's head. By the time Martha regained consciousness, the shooting had stopped. "The savages are leaving," one of the men called. Martha sat very still, as if in a daze.

"They'll be back," Thomas Ireland said with certainty.

"What Indians attacked us?" one of the women, Julia Wright, asked as if she could not believe the settlers' sudden peril.

"It was White Lodge and Lean Bear's bands," Thomas Ireland answered. "I saw them before they saw me, thank God. I was heading back to the house after milking my cow when I saw them coming through my corn field. I thought there was something odd about the way they were dressed. The last time I saw those chiefs and their lazy followers was when I visited their camp at Shakotan. They were wearing government issue clothes then and looked tame and peaceable." He shook his head. "But now they're stripped for war. Their hair is tied back and war paint is all over their faces and bodies. When I saw them, I ran for the house, got my family out, and then went to warn the Duleys."

"But White Lodge is an old man," Mrs. Ireland protested. "Why should he be going to war?"

Thomas moved to where his wife and two little girls sat huddled together on the floor. "We should have paid more attention to the rumors of how unsettled the Santee were. They've been discontented ever since their annuities didn't show up. We should've noticed when they quit trading for food and their squaws and children came to beg."

William Duley nodded in agreement. "Only yesterday two squaws came begging for eggs. Remember, Martha?" he asked his wife anxiously trying to distract her from the stupor that still gripped her.

"Yes," Julia Wright answered instead. "They came to our place, too. I felt sorry for them. Their men can't find game to hunt; their gardens didn't do well, and they were depending on their annuities for survival."

"But why should they want to kill us?" Martha suddenly demanded, almost screaming. "It isn't our fault!"

"Shush, Martha," William tried to comfort her, and Sarah patted her mother's arm. Martha began to cry and William Duley spoke more sternly, "Martha, you must try to calm yourself. You're frightening the children."

The other settlers were silent, having no answer to the hysterical woman's question. The men began to plan their defense. They didn't have much ammunition, but they were sure the stout cabin would keep the Indians from overwhelming them for a long time. There was food and water in the big cabin, they told each other reassuringly, but the men knew that they could not last for too many days. The provisions and ammunition would have to be carefully rationed.

The lookout men at the windows called out that the Indians had retreated to the woods and seemed to be holding a council.

"What do you suppose they're up to?" Wright wondered in the quiet that followed the Indians' retreat.

"I don't know," answered Duley, "but I expect they're planning to rush us. We'd better be ready."

Nothing happened for a long time. The men still watched at the window, but the women relaxed a little and calmed the children and tried to make themselves more comfortable as they waited.

"Here comes Pawn," John Wright called out from his post at the window.

The others crowded to see. A lone old Indian, Pawn, who had often camped in Wright's yard, was approaching the cabin waving a white flag.

"He's coming closer. Shall we let him in?" someone asked.

"He's not armed," John Wright said, watching the Indian's cautious progress. "Let's see what he wants." He opened the door, swiftly pulled Pawn inside, and slammed the bolt back into place.

The settlers were not afraid of the old man who, with his few followers, had been a frequent visitor to the Shetek settlement. They thought he was simple-minded and harmless because of his constant foolish smile. Pawn was trembling as he stumbled into their midst.

"He's scared," William Duley said as he took the Indian's arm to steady the old man.

Pawn nodded and gave a weak grin, but stammered

as he spoke. "*Han*," he grunted. "Pawn 'fraid. White Lodge kill Pawn if Pawn help settlers," his eyes rolled fearfully. "White Lodge say you go. No kill whites if all leave Indian land. If you not go, White Lodge burn big lodge and kill everybody." He fell silent and the settlers looked at him in amazement. Pawn's speech was the longest he had ever made.

"White Lodge gone now," Pawn went on. "Take bad Indians to fight whites at Yellow Medicine. You," he said, indicating all of the settlers, "go swamp. Hide tall grass. Bad Indians come back tonight. Burn big lodge."

"What do you think?" the men asked each other as they considered Pawn's suggestion.

"I think he's right," Thomas Ireland said. "The slough would be a good place to hide. We could put the women and children in the center, and the men would be better able to pick off the Indians if they attacked. We'll have a better chance to defend ourselves than if we waited and tried to fight our way out of a burning cabin."

"Right," William Duley agreed. "And in the shelter of the tall grass one of us could sneak away to get help."

The others agreed. Some of the men would leave the cabin first, then the women and children. The rest of the men would follow to protect the retreat to the slough. The women and children would hide in the dense, tall reeds and the armed men would arrange themselves in a protective ring. They lined up at the door.

John Wright peered out and then grabbed Pawn and shoved the old Indian out. "You go first," he cried, wanting to make sure there was no ambush.

No shots came as the old man stumbled out, and Wright led the rush to the swamp. The settlers all reached the slough before they heard the war whoops of the encircling Santee.

Sarah heard her father call, "Run!" and she stumbled through the rough grass toward the thicker cover of the tall reeds. She pulled the wailing Nancy with her.

The settlers were running wildly to the center of the slough, but they were slowed by the thick reeds and the muck of the swamp, and the Indian arrows and bullets that were cutting them down. Sarah saw her father follow Pawn who was running for the shelter of the woods. He shot Pawn in the back and turned as Sarah yelled a warning, but too late. He went down unconscious under the club of a near-naked brave.

Sarah was weeping as she and Nancy stumbled on.

"Sarah! Sarah!" she heard Billy scream and she turned to see her brother holding tightly to Robert's hand, running along the edge of the slough. The boys were followed by a warrior brandishing a war axe, and Sarah screamed as first Robert and then Billy were felled, blood bursting from their small shattered heads.

"No! No!" Sarah wept as she fell to her knees in the damp grass and hugged Nancy to her.

"Get up!" Julia Wright ordered, coming behind the girls carrying her son. "Get into the tall grass." The woman jerked Nancy after her, but Sarah saw her mother running to where the two boys lay dead and could not move.

"Mama!" Sarah screamed as she saw her mother fall after a pursuing brave shot her in the foot.

Sarah could not stand it any more. She jumped to her feet and ran to where her mother was desperately crawling toward the boys' bodies. The girl reached the edge of the slough and then felt an Indian grab her skirts. She jerked away and stumbled, and then her head snapped back as the warrior flipped her by her long braids onto the ground. Again, she got away and tried to run to where her mother was down on the ground struggling with a laughing brave. She heard a shot and felt sudden pain in her left arm; she was spun around and then fell on her back. She struggled to rise and screamed in terror as a dark, painted face loomed above her. Sarah scratched, kicked and bit at the Indian, whose teeth gleamed in a grotesque smile. A sharp blow in her belly knocked the wind out of her. She gasped for air as she felt a smothering weight upon her, and then she knew nothing.

When Sarah awoke, the screams of the settlers, the murderous howls of the Indians, and the gun shots were stilled. She heard only the quiet sobbing of Nancy, who clung tightly to her sister's right hand. Sarah struggled to sit up and cried aloud when she put her weight on the hand of her shattered arm. Almost fainting from the pain she lay back on the ground until her head cleared, and then tried again. Nancy helped her, and Sarah sat up and looked around.

Nancy's hair was straggling over her face and her clothes were torn, but she seemed unharmed. Julia Wright was sitting against a tree; her eyes were closed and she was rocking her five-year old Johnny. Mary and Sally Ireland, eight and nine years, held tightly to each other. Nine-year old Lillie Everett crawled to Julia Wright and snuggled against her—the only adult comfort she could find.

Sarah saw that the small group was sitting near the

edge of the oak grove near the big cabin. She looked around in confusion for she had no recollection of returning to the place. She saw an Indian warrior sitting a little ways off apparently guarding the woman and children, but his eyes were on the larger party of Indians who were busily looting the Wright cabin.

Sarah looked away. Julia Wright opened her eyes and put one arm around the Everett girl. She saw that Sarah was awake and asked sadly, "Are you all right, child?"

"I—I hurt all over," Sarah whimpered from a raw throat, "especially my arm." She looked down at herself and to her horror found that only a remnant of cloth covered her nakedness. Her throbbing arm had been wrapped with a strip torn from her skirt. "How did we get here?" she asked.

"The Indians found us after searching for survivors in the swamp and brought us here," Julia explained wearily.

Tears came to Sarah as she remembered her brothers' deaths. "Pa? Mama?" she asked fearfully.

"I saw your father crawling into the slough after he'd been clubbed. I don't know if he made it or not," Julia answered and then pointed to a spot behind where the Duley girls sat. "There's your mother."

Sarah turned and saw Martha Duley lying on the ground. "Is she dead?"

"No," Julia said, "she's sleeping. I don't think she wants to wake up."

Sarah and Nancy moved to their mother. Sarah began rubbing her limp wrists, and Nancy took her mother's hand and cried, "Mama, wake up!"

The girls' pleading finally made Martha open her eyes. She stared dazedly at her daughters, and Sarah could see that she was fighting the pain of her wounded foot and battered body. Martha moaned and her eyes glazed, as if she were drawing a protective curtain over her mind. Sarah was frightened, for she knew how easily her mother could withdraw into herself when faced with unpleasantness. "Mama, mama," she called desperately.

But it was little Nancy who brought her mother to awareness. She cradled her head on Martha's breast and clung tightly. The pleading touch of the child roused the woman and she sat up. She began to weep when she saw Sarah's wound and her nearly naked body. The three clung to each other and found comfort in each other's nearness. At last Martha looked around and noticed Julia Wright and the other children.

"Julia," she called, "are we all that's left?"

"I don't know," Julia answered sadly. "The Indians are still looking through the swamp. They said they wouldn't kill any more of us if we surrendered. You and Sarah," Julia went on, "looked like you were dead, but Nancy wouldn't leave you until I made sure. When I knew that you were alive, I convinced the Indians to bring you along."

"William?" Martha asked.

"The last time I saw William, he was alive. He and my John wanted to go for help, but I didn't see John again after I went into the slough. I hope he made it," she sighed.

"I think Mrs. Eastlick is still alive," Julia went on. "She got hit over the head, but I saw her move before I came out of the swamp. She may have feigned death when the Indians found her. Some of the others may still be hiding in the tall grass—I don't know. It was all so confusing. But we—" she waved her hand at the children, Martha, and herself— "are prisoners of the Indians."

"Oh, no," Martha moaned, and Sarah held her mother closer. "What's going to happen to us?" the girl asked Julia.

"I don't know," the woman answered, shaking her head. Suddenly she stiffened and Sarah followed her gaze to where several warriors rode through the oak trees from the swamp. The other Indians came from the cabin and gathered around, and Sarah saw that they were arguing. A man and a woman left the group and approached the survivors. The Indian guarding them stood to meet them.

Sarah saw that the Santee braves were clothed in strange combinations of apparel that had once belonged to the Shetek settlers. One of the men had forced his arms through the sleeves of a red blouse which Sarah recognized as having been part of Mrs. Ireland's best dress. The other Santee wore white man's trousers; a bloody scalp dangled from its belt loops.

The Indian woman accompanying the man had tied around herself a blue skirt that was clearly some white woman's gown. It dragged on the ground as she walked. A green strip of cloth was tied around her braided white hair, and a settler's patchwork quilt covered her stooped shoulders. She gave a toothless grin to Julia and Martha and clucked sympathetically over the children. "Me, Anna," she said. "Me go Mission school. Learn white talk." She smiled again and pointed to where the Indians were preparing themselves and their horses to leave the settlement. "We go now. Can't wait to find more whites who alive," Anna said as she motioned for the prisoners to rise. "Soldiers might come."

Sarah and Nancy helped their mother struggle to

her feet as Anna handed Martha a rude crutch fashioned from a tree limb. The Indians were in a hurry, and some had already started moving westward. Sarah and Julia were given bulky packs bound together with ropes, and the Indian woman strapped them onto their backs.

Martha could barely hobble even with the crutch, and when a pack was strapped on her back too, she stumbled and fell. The Indian woman yelled at her and hit her over the head, but Martha remained on the ground, impervious to the blow. Anna seized Martha's arm and jerked her upright. She handed Martha the crutch and pushed her forward. Sarah and Nancy supported their mother to keep her from falling as the Indians moved out. The two Ireland girls, as well as Lillie Everett and Nancy, were considered to be too young to carry packs; they walked close by the other survivors.

Most of the Santee women also walked with heavy packs on their backs, and their children followed. Only the warriors, the very old, and the young toddlers were permitted to ride the few horses of the band. Slowly, the Santee moved in a long procession in a westerly direction.

Sarah was worried about her mother, who hobbled along as if she were in a stupor. She fell often and each time received a blow and a rough command from Anna as the girls helped their mother up. Soon they fell behind the others. When Martha fell again, the Indian woman disgustedly removed the white woman's pack, gave her a kick, and ordered the girls to leave their mother.

"No," Sarah said firmly, trying not to cry. "Let us help her up again."

"No!" Anna yelled, pushing the wailing Nancy ahead and tugging on Sarah's good arm. "Leave crippled woman. She hold Santee back. Santee hurry. Get away before soldiers come!"

Sarah pulled away from Anna. Nancy had already run back to her mother, and both girls were now weeping loudly.

The brave who was wearing Mrs. Ireland's blouse heard the girls' wails and rode back to investigate. He saw the white woman crumpled on the ground with her daughters hovering over her and gave an angry shout. He lashed down at Anna with his quirt and ordered her to help Martha mount his horse. Anna did so, grumbling loudly in Dakota, but fearing his anger. As the brave rode off with Martha behind him, Anna explained, with a leer and a toothless smile, the man's intention.

"My son, Stands High, take cripple for wife," she

giggled. She laughed even more at the look of horror on Sarah and Julia's faces. "You be wife of brave, too," she told the shocked Julia. "And maybe even young squaw with shining hair," she said to Sarah.

Sarah felt a cramp in her stomach and turned aside and retched. Julia Wright put her arm around the girl. "Come," she said gently, "do not be afraid. You are too young to be a wife. That ugly woman was trying to scare us with a bad joke." She led Sarah on. Nancy and little Johnny followed.

The Santee marched with the sun, and as it neared the horizon they stopped in a sheltered glen along a winding river. The captives were herded together again. Sarah and Nancy went to their mother, who stared straight ahead with unseeing eyes. They were joined by the Indian woman, Anna, who led them to a tipi. Anna motioned for them to enter and sit. Inside she poked around in a leather case and produced a comb and some small tin trade boxes.

"Braid hair like Anna," she said holding out the comb to Julia.

Sarah relaxed. Her long blond, nearly white, hair and that of Nancy's needed grooming, as did all of the captives. Julia Wright took the comb and began pulling it through the snarls of Lillie Everett's hair.

"Wait," commanded Anna. "Oil hair first." She

smiled as she scooped a handful of rancid tallow from one of the tins and smeared it over Lillie's head. "You Dakota now," she explained. "Be pretty like Anna. And oil keep bugs away."

The captives made no response. Julia Wright groomed the hair of Lillie Everett and the little Ireland girls before she did her own. Anna took the comb and ran it through Johnny's oiled hair. "No cut boy's hair no more," she said to Julia. "He soon be Dakota warrior."

Anna offered the comb to Martha, but Sarah took it, since her mother made no move to do so. The girl dabbed tallow on Nancy's head and tears came as she braided her little sister's hair. Her thoughts went back to the morning, which seemed so long ago, when Nancy had wanted to leave yesterday's braids in today. Sarah combed her mother's hair and then finally her own which, when oiled with the tallow, hung in two stiff clubs down her back.

The Indian woman then put the comb away and opened a tin of red paint. "Like this," she demonstrated dipping her finger into the vermilion and smearing it down the part on Lillie Everett's head. Each captive, except Johnny Wright, had her scalp painted the same way. Then from another tin Anna smeared a brown, oily dye over everyone's face. She stood back when she had finished, looked over their darkened faces carefully, and grunted in approval. Sarah guessed that this had been done so their white faces would not be conspicuous among the Indians.

Anna rummaged in a pile of ragged clothing taken from the Shetek settlers' homes and indicated that the captives were to clothe themselves. "Once," she said sadly, "the Santee were wealthy. We wore rich skins. New wives and daughters dressed good. No more," she said shaking her head.

She scowled fiercely upon the captives. "You stay," she ordered and turned to leave the tipi. "Me bring food."

Soon she returned with a small cast iron kettle and ladled out a savory soup into crude wooden bowls and passed them to the captives. The younger children hungrily ate their first food of the day. Sarah was ravenous but took a sip reluctantly. She found it delicious, but she was suspicious of what kind of meat she was eating. "Good cow," Anna said, and then Sarah ate.

"Eat, Martha," Julia Wright urged. "We must keep up our strength, and you need the nourishment so your foot will heal." Martha roused herself and took a little of the soup.

After they had eaten, Anna left the captives alone

for the night after telling them not to try to escape. "Some Santee want to kill you," she warned.

When they were alone, Julia bathed Martha's shattered foot with the water Anna had left. She bound the wound as best as she could with a bandage made from the ragged clothes. She also cleansed and rebandaged Sarah's wounded arm.

It was late evening now. The children huddled around the women and, except for Sarah, were all soon asleep. Her arm ached and visions of the day's horrors kept swirling through her mind. To shut them out she concentrated on the sounds coming from the Indian camp. Barking dogs were quickly silenced by male voices; crying babies and quarreling women were sharply hushed by a gutteral command. Soon the night settling noises of the Santee were stilled, and Sarah succumbed to the weariness of her young, abused body.

Early the next morning the captives were awakened by Anna who gave them cold remnants of the previous night's meat and then ordered them to dismantle the tipi. While Julia struggled with the unfamiliar task, Anna poked at Martha. Sarah and Nancy helped their mother rise, and they clumsily tried to help Julia. Anna stood laughing at their efforts until Stands High, the brave in the red shirt, came and admonished her to hurry. Anna then showed the captives how to strike the tipi, fold it, and place it on the waiting horse.

Stands High returned and again Martha was permitted to ride behind him. Sarah, with a pack on her back, and Nancy were ordered to tag along after the horse.

An Indian woman about Anna's age came up, and after much gesticulating and giggling interpretation from Anna, told Julia Wright that she was now the third wife of the chief, White Lodge. Julia would have the honor of leading one of the chief's horses, and her son could ride.

Julia gave Sarah a quick pat on the shoulder before she followed the old woman away. "Be strong, Sarah," she whispered. "Your mother and little Nancy need you."

The two Ireland girls, their fingers in their mouths, were led away by another Indian woman who was happily smiling. "Trembling Hand," Anna explained, pointing to the departing squaw, "is happy. Adopt girls. Own daughters died in winter."

Lillie Everett was adopted by another Indian woman who had three sons but no daughters.

Sarah watched the little girls being petted and wept over, and wondered about the man who had claimed the Duley family. "Why does that man take us?" she asked Anna, pointing to the red-shirted brave.

"Stands High wife and daughters die in hungry winter. He have only old mother, Anna. You new family."

"You mean we will be living with you?" Sarah asked.

Anna nodded and hurried them after her son's horse.

"Why does the chief take Julia?" Nancy wanted to know, trotting to keep up and jealous that little John Wright got to ride.

"White Lodge has one old wife. Has stiff knees. Can't work good. Second wife going have baby. Chief needs new wife to care for him. He proud to have white son." She motioned Nancy to be still. "No more talk. Santee must hurry."

The Indians moved out to the north, following the river, which Anna told Sarah was the Big Sioux, and they began long days of travel and new camps in new places. In the days and weeks that followed, the band moved steadily north and away from Minnesota. Sarah's arm healed cleanly, but it stayed stiff at the elbow and she could not bend it. Despite her handicap, she and Nancy assisted Martha with the work of the lodge of Stands High. Martha existed in a stupor and made no protest when Nancy soon began playing happily with Indian children or when both of her daughters began speaking Dakota. Sarah realized sadly that her mother cared for nothing, not even the welfare of her children.

Occasionally Martha was prodded back to awareness by Julia, who visited them during the evening stops. Julia tried to explain her new status to Martha and Sarah. As the wife of the chief, her lot and that of her son had improved.

"It's not so bad," she told the Duleys. "White Lodge's old wife can't do much and the younger wife is clumsy with child, so I have to do most of the work, but he has been good to us."

She looked with pity at Martha, whose head was cradled in Sarah's good arm. "If you would only try . . ." she pleaded. "Sarah's doing all of your work. If it weren't for Anna, your daughters would suffer terribly." She turned to Sarah, who had grown taller and thinner, "Can't you make her understand?"

Sarah shook her head and her tears fell on her mother's head. She knew that Martha had ceased to listen and had withdrawn into a state which protected her from the horrors of memory and knowledge of the present.

III

White Lodge

Wakeyeska, whom the white people called White Lodge, sat musing unhappily in front of the center fire in the sparse comfort of his tipi. Once his lodge had been that of a rich man, furnished with warm buffalo robes, parfleches stuffed with food, and an always-full tobacco pouch. Now, after a meager meal of squirrel his stomach grumbled and angrily he put away his empty pipe. His old wife lay snoring in her place near the fire, wrapped in a thin issue blanket. The younger wife, Yellow Leaf, was warm in his second-best buffalo robe; White Lodge had given it to her because she carried the growing seed of his old age. He kept the warmest and best robe for himself, as was proper for his station and years, and now he sat wrapped in the newest issue blanket.

White Lodge ignored the women in his tipi until his new wife moved to replenish the dying fire before she lay down beside her sleeping son. From the corner of his eye, White Lodge saw Yellow Leaf stick out her foot so that Julia tripped and almost stumbled into the glowing embers. The old man growled a warning at the women. He knew Yellow Leaf was jealous of his white wife, but tonight he wanted no women squabble to distract him.

Still, he was distracted when Julia smiled gratefully at him as she lay down on the sleeping robe she shared with him. White Lodge did not return the smile, but his heart softened as he watched the white woman. Julia was a good wife. She had quickly learned the intricacies of setting up the lodge and dismantling it so that White Lodge's old wife with stiff bones could search immediately for roots and berries with other old women when a new camp was made. The white wife carried wood and water so that Yellow Leaf, awkward with her soon-to-be-born child, could busy herself with the cooking. White Lodge's tipi was well-organized because of the addition of Julia.

From Julia, White Lodge's thoughts moved to the

other captives and he frowned. There were some among the band who wanted the whites killed or abandoned on the trail, for the captives were eating food needed by the Santee. But the mothers who had adopted white children fiercely protected their charges and claimed that the children were fast becoming good Santee. All spoke Dakota and helped with the camp chores. The only captive who was a hindrance to the band was the Duley woman. White Lodge frowned again. The woman, taken by Stands High, was mad, but was harmless. Her daughters, especially Sarah who was called Shining Hair, protected their mother, and Anna, Stands High's mother, shielded the girls. Stands High himself ignored the laughter of the other Santee men who made fun of him for having a crazy woman.

White Lodge sighed. He knew that soon he would have to deal with the problem of what to do with the captives. He pulled his blanket closer and glanced longingly at Julia who lay on his sleeping robe. He was pleased with his captive wife, and she kept him warm at night. Resolutely he removed thoughts of her from his mind. He could not seek warmth for his old bones yet. He must sit alone while his household slept until he decided where next to lead his people.

The eighty lodges of the Santee camp, which was

made up of White Lodge's band and the followers of the dead Lean Bear, were in trouble. The provisions they had taken from the Lake Shetek settlers had lasted about four weeks. During that time there had been plenty to eat and the warriors did no hunting, nor did the women fish in any of the streams where they had camped.

The fear of pursuit had lessened as the Santee traveled north, but they had had to leave the lovely valley of the Big Sioux. From the summit of the river's bluffs the undulating prairie could be viewed for miles around, and a band of fleeing Indians could be spotted easily by any following soldiers. After leaving the Big Sioux, the Santee had moved north into the Dakota territory where few white men ventured. The captured provisions were exhausted by then, and the band lived on the edible roots the women found and whatever animals or wild fowl the hunters got. Many of the horses had died, leaving more of the people on foot, but providing needed meat.

When the Santee reached the Elm River, the people were in need of rest as well as food. On the Elm, a Yanktonais camp was discovered, and White Lodge had made overtures to join the village which seemed to have plenty. But he had been rejected. The Yanktonais wanted no part of the Minnesota Santee battle even if it were only to provide shelter to a fleeing band. Neither did the Yanktonais want white captives in their midst; they feared retribution by angry white soldiers. The Santee were allowed to stay one night and were given a little corn. Then White Lodge had to leave. He hurried his people southwest to the James River.

Here, on the west bank of the James, White Lodge had hoped to make a secure winter camp. The narrow, deep, clear river water was good to drink, there was wild fowl and squirrels, and perhaps buffalo on the prairies further west. The river's banks had thick groves of timber to provide shelter from the winter winds and fuel for the tipis' fires. But now, White Lodge mused bitterly, this good place would have to be abandoned.

Last night a weary Santee warrior had ridden into White Lodge's camp. He was Speaks Fire, the emissary of Little Crow, returning from an unsuccessful mission on the Missouri to enlist the aid of the Teton. White Lodge had fed the tired, dispirited warrior and given him a sleeping robe for the night. In the morning the chief summoned the Council to hear what Speaks Fire had to tell.

Before the Council gathered a runner announced

the visit of two more Santee warriors. These men were fleeing from Minnesota where they had fought with Little Crow. They brought the unhappy news of their leader's defeat and the capture of many Santee warriors, whose women and children had been either murdered by vengeful whites or made prisoner. The Uprising, so optimistically begun to rid the land of the whites, was over. White Lodge and his band, and all of the Santee, were fugitives.

When Little Crow's emissary, Speaks Fire, heard the news, he had raged bitterly against the Teton. "The time for united effort is lost!" he cried. "The Two Kettles would not help us." He beat mournfully upon his breast. "Some of them were for us, but others would punish us—punish their cousins, who are starving, for trespassing upon their buffalo lands. Others wept because we killed the whites or took them captive, as you have, White Lodge."

White Lodge had added his *"Ho"* of agreement and the emissary raged on. "But they, the Two Kettles and all of the Teton, were afraid. They were afraid that if they went to war with us the white traders would leave and they would lose their barter goods. They would not even give us, their hungry cousins, food or shelter, for fear the white soldiers would punish them!"

The emissary wept, *"Hinh, hinh,"* and White

Lodge had averted his head so as not to see the man's tears. "*Witkokoka!*" the unhappy warrior had stormed in his anguish, "Fools! They could not see that if our peoples, the whole of the Dakota, united we could drive the whites away forever. Now," he sighed, "it is too late. Taoya Te Duta, Little Crow, is defeated. Too late. But they will see," he said as he rose to leave the council tipi, "the Teton will know the loss of their lands and of the treachery of the whites. They will long for allies then, but the Santee will be scattered to the winds."

The Council rose and followed Speaks Fire out to his waiting horse. He mounted, covered his face with his blanket in sorrow, and rode off with the two Little Crow warriors to join their chief in exile. The women began their wailing and the camp grieved.

White Lodge remembered all these sad things as he sat awake in the chilling night before his dying fire. He wished one of the women would wake and replenish the wood, but he did not wake them. He pulled his blanket closer over his white head and weary shoulders. Ruefully he recalled how briefly fired with energy he had been as he fought as well as a young man in the battle at Lake Shetek. He had even a youth's desire to take a new wife. But now he felt old, tired, and full of sorrow.

It was the Moon When Dead Leaves Are Snapping

and Shaken Off by the Wind, a time when the people should have been settled in a winter camp with provisions to last till spring. They had hunted little game as they fled into Dakota. Now, with Little Crow's defeat, White Lodge could not return to his home at Shakotan where a little corn was cached and there was at least fish to eat.

The old man sighed and again tightened his blanket as he heard the wind howling at the smoke hole and making the fire jump into brief flame. There was a hint of snow in the sound. He must find a winter camp where food and clothing could be provided for the people. Yet, he could not stay here on the James. It was still too close to Minnesota and the danger of pursuit. He would have to go farther west. Yes, White Lodge nodded to himself, he would lead his people along the old buffalo trail which ended at the mouth of the Beaver on the Missouri River in the north Dakota land, where there were no white settlers. The mouth of the Beaver would be a good winter camp site. Once it had been a good place for buffalo and antelope—maybe the game would still be there—and if he did not bother the Teton they would let him stay.

White Lodge gave a great yawn, sleepy now that he had reached a decision. He moved to where Julia lay on the sleeping robe and pulled his blanket and the buffalo robe over himself and the woman. Soon his snores joined those of his wife.

The northwest wind danced over the tipi poles of Santee lodges, indiscriminately ducking down smoke flaps, breathing fires into feeble flame, and scattering ashes of dead embers. In the lodge of Stands High, Sarah Duley stirred restlessly under the thin blanket she shared with her sister. She was cold and her stiff elbow ached with the chill. The tipi was filled with the sleep sounds of Stands High and his mother, Anna, who had insisted the girls call her *Kunśi*, grandmother.

Sarah lay still, listening, hoping that Kunśi would awaken and rekindle the dead fire. Sarah knew her mother, who lived in a constant state of dull insensibility, would never do it, and starting a fresh fire with tinder and flint was difficult for the girl because of her crippled arm. But when Kunśi's snores rumbled on, Sarah sat up. She shivered in her cotton shift and crawled to the center fire after gathering twigs and a small log from the pile near the door. It was nearly dawn and the tipi's interior was filled with enough gray light for the girl to find her way easily. She moved her hands exploringly through the still-warm ashes and then jerked away when her fingers touched a live coal. Quickly she blew upon it, ignoring the ashes which flew into her face, and as the ember flared she piled kindling twigs over it. Soon it was a living fire, and Sarah gratefully turned her aching arm to its soothing warmth.

She sensed that someone was watching. Sarah turned and saw that her mother was awake and for once had a gleam of consciousness in her eyes. Sarah's heart jumped happily when Martha gave her a gentle smile. But the smile froze on Martha's face when Stands High muttered and coughed in his sleep next to her. The unseeing glaze returned to Martha's eyes, and Sarah knew that her mother's moment of lucidness was gone.

Sarah shivered and crawled back to Nancy; she cuddled against the little girl and pulled the blanket tightly over them. Warm again and almost asleep, she heard the distant high honking of southward-flying geese. The sound was so mournful in the pre-dawn's stillness that Sarah was filled with unbearable loneliness. Her mother was a helpless imbecile. Her sister carelessly played with Indian children, chattering in Dakota, and had forgotten civilized ways. There was no one to comfort the unhappy young girl who yearned bitterly for the strong presence of her father and the laughter of her dead brothers. The geese calls ceased as the flock settled into a pot hole near the river, and the girl slept even as tears formed in the corners of her eyes.

White Lodge heard the geese, too, but to him it was a good sound. He roused his women who built up the fire and prepared his morning meat. He ordered the boy, Johnny, to fetch his eldest son, Black Hawk. When Black Hawk came into his father's tipi, grumbling at the early rising, White Lodge sent him immediately out to wake the hunters. The geese were flying south, and next to buffalo the Santee dearly loved the wild fowl's flesh.

For two days the hunters brought in the heavy honkers. The women could hardly keep up with their plucking and skinning. Moccasins and cradle boards were lined with warm down, whole skins were tanned for warm caps. The Santee gorged themselves on the rich goose meat and saved the fat to use as healing ointment for winter coughs and aching limbs.

On the morning of the third day, White Lodge led his people southwest on the buffalo trail. The Santee moved out in happy order. The sun was high, the wind was still, and for the first week the march was easy. Then the smoked goose was gone, the hunters found no buffalo, and the Santee suffered as they turned into the northwest wind.

The captives, clad only in ragged cotton garments and wrapped in thin blankets, were in agony. Julia

Wright's shoes had been taken by Yellow Feather, and the white woman had little feeling in her feet as she walked. Stands High was one of the hunters assigned to range far on either side of the moving band in search of game, so Martha Duley had to walk. She fell often as she hobbled along on her crutch. Sarah and Nancy helped their mother, but each time she fell it was harder to get her to her feet. They were in danger of falling far behind the main column. The Santee who passed them shouted out that they could not wait for the crippled, mad white woman. "Leave her," they called to the girls and Anna who walked with the captives.

Anna made no attempt to help Martha, but she sharply rebuked the Santee who wanted to abandon the white woman. When Martha went down again and the weary girls could not get her up, Anna shouted at them, "You will die, if you stay behind!" She motioned to the treeless plains they traveled. "No water. No shelter. Bad country. Only Indian know how to live here."

But Martha made no effort to help herself, and her exhausted daughters wept. Anna angrily jerked Sarah away from her mother. "Go to White Lodge's new wife. She please White Lodge. Tell her 'bout . . . ," she motioned to Martha.

Sarah ran after the Santee band. She found Julia marching with White Lodge's family at the head of the column. Breathlessly she told of Martha's plight. Julia hurried to White Lodge, who rode at the head of the march.

"My husband," she addressed him formally and used for the first time the title which acknowledged her relationship to the chief. Julia swallowed, her throat constricted over the repugnant words, but she spoke them again in a louder voice. "My husband, a favor."

White Lodge looked down at his white wife walking beside his horse. He was pleased with her respectful manner of address. "*Ho*, woman," he answered as he rode, "what do you wish?"

"My sister, the mother of Shining Hair," Julia began slowly, searching for the appropriate Dakota words, "can not ride because her husband, Stands High, is among the hunters. She falls far behind the rest."

White Lodge frowned and Julia hurried on. "Will my husband be kind, as he always is as a great chief, and show mercy to the white woman?"

"What will you have me do?" White Lodge growled.

"Let her ride behind one of your other wives."

White Lodge's two Santee wives heard Julia's request and protested loudly. "My horse carries many packs beside myself. There is not room for another rider," said his old wife.

"And I have arranged my packs so that the child will not be harmed as I ride," proclaimed the pregnant Yellow Feather.

"Be still!" White Lodge commanded. He detested quarreling among his women. "If the baggage can be carried by other means," he said to Julia, "the white woman may ride behind my first wife."

The old wife grumbled loudly, but White Lodge again commanded her to be quiet. "Go," he said to Julia. "Do not disturb me further!"

Julia hurriedly led the horse carrying the still-grumbling old woman back to where Nancy and Anna waited beside Martha. She distributed the packs of household gear among herself and Sarah. Even Nancy was given a cooking pot to carry. Anna watched grumblingly, but then, seeing how burdened Sarah was, she took some of the extra weight from the girl's back. "You fall behind if back too full," she complained.

The women and girls moved up to join White Lodge's family and there were many loud complaints from the Santee they passed.

The passage across the Dakota prairie became more

difficult for the band. There was nothing to break the cold wind and there was heavy frost over the tipis each morning. The women twisted the tall prairie grass into tight bundles to burn for fuel as there were no buffalo chips to gather. The hunters ranged far on either side of the moving villagers, but found only an occasional jack rabbit for the cook pots and the women watched for gophers and field mice as they marched.

As the Santee became weary and hungry more and more of them became unwilling to share their sparse fare with the captives. The Santee mothers who had adopted the white children still protected their charges, but they were thwarted when food was distributed. Even White Lodge gave less to Julia and her son and Julia was given the responsibility for keeping the night fire fed with the grass twists. She got little sleep because the grass burned quickly and if she, in her exhaustion, let the fire die, White Lodge allowed his Santee wives to beat her.

In the lodge of Stands High, the night fire duty fell on Sarah. The weak, weary girl often let the tipi get cold and not even Anna could stop the angry blows Stands High gave the child. But Anna was skilled at filching extra food and managed to keep her household fed.

As the interminable march continued, Sarah and

Julia tried to encourage the other captives, but they feared for all their lives.

At last the hungry people reached the mouth of the Beaver. The women fanned out along the stream to gather the dried remnants of choke cherries and wild plums still clinging to the leafless bushes. They picked rose hips, and dug into the hard earth bare-handed or with pointed sticks to salvage the last of the *tipsina*. But even with wood to burn, the Beaver was a disappointing winter camp site. There was no buffalo. The pronghorns and deer seemed to have vanished. The people were starving and White Lodge was desperate. Where could he go now?

Again the old man sat staring into the center fire, which burned in the daytime now in the Moon When the Deer Lost Their Horns. White Lodge's thoughts were unhappy as he cast about in his mind for a better location for a winter camp. A young brave interrupted the chief's thoughts by rushing into the tipi without any polite throat-clearing before he entered.

"A boat is coming down the river," he cried before White Lodge could reprimand him for bad manners. "There are white men and an Indian woman in the boat!"

White Lodge rose and led the way out of the tipi. He did not notice Julia's startled expression when she heard the brave's message, nor did he see her follow. He was too excited. Perhaps the boat held a party of white trappers setting their snares along the river. No matter who the white men were, they would have supplies which White Lodge's people desperately needed.

Julia mingled with the villagers who had heard the news of the boat and moved toward the river. She slipped away from the large group and hid herself in brush along the shore some distance downstream from where White Lodge watched the boat approaching.

The chief was thwarted. He had no canoes to intercept the boat as it moved down the center of the river; he would have to lure the white men to shore. He gave his orders to the young warriors, who quickly ran to hide in the brush. White Lodge and a few of the old men waited in plain sight on the bank. The rest of the curious Santee were ordered back to camp.

The white men gesticulated to each other when they spotted White Lodge. He held up his hand in the peace sign and waved for them to come in. He watched while the white men discussed what to do and saw that the Indian woman was trying to dissuade them from going to shore. White Lodge growled to himself. He would like to have his hands about the treacherous woman's neck. He let out a grunt of relief as the boat swung toward him.

As the boat neared, one of the white men stood up and hailed the Indians. "Who are you?" he called in rough Dakota.

White Lodge motioned to one of his old men, who answered, "A peaceful hunting party who wish to trade. Who are you?"

"I am Major Galpin and these are a party of miners. We are on our way downstream to Fort Randall." He threw a long line to shore and one of the Santee secured it to a tree.

When Major Galpin stepped on to the shore, White Lodge signaled the hidden warriors. Whooping and brandishing their weapons, some of the braves stood on the rope to hold the boat to the shore. But the woman in the craft was even quicker. As White Lodge yelled a warning to his men, he saw the flash of the woman's axe as it severed the line. The Major jumped back into the boat; it tipped dangerously beneath him, then righted and gained momentum as it reached the main channel. The occupants of the boat lay flat on the bottom as the Santee arrows whirred harmlessly over their heads.

White Lodge shouted angrily for his men to follow the boat along the bank. He followed the yelling warriors, then stopped incredulously as he heard a woman's screams above the noise of pursuit. It was his new wife, the white woman, yelling to the men in the boat.

"Help!" Julia called desperately as the boat moved downstream. "There are two white women and six children captive here! Please! Help! Mrs. Duley, Mrs. Wright, our chil—" Her frantic plea was shut off by a rough hand clamped tightly over her mouth, and the arm around her waist jerked her out of sight into the sheltering brush.

Julia screamed, and bit, clawed and kicked at the warrior who carried her to the chief. She had one brief glimpse of White Lodge's face contorted with rage before his heavy fist struck her full in the face.

IV

Fool Soldiers

The Two Kettles were settled into their village for the winter. The fall hunt had been good even if the young men had had to range far to find the decreasing buffalo herds. Every tipi that had a hunter was well supplied with dried meat and warm buffalo robes. The lodges of the old, widowed and orphaned were given plenty and there were robes left over to barter to the traders for blankets, cooking pots, coffee, sugar, and ammunition. There were fat, strong horses in the herd, enough mounts so that no one need walk. The Two Kettle village was a rich one and they would winter in comfort.

It was the month which the Teton called Moon

When Winter Sets In, and the young men were restless. There was no need to hunt or to steal more horses. There was no opportunity to make war, to count *coup* or to show their courage and fully become men.

Waanatan, The Charger, and his brother-friend, Kills And Comes, were among the restless ones. They had returned successful from their vision quest and now had the respect of the tribe, but their valor was unproven. Their journey to and from the buttes with Swift Bear had taken two weeks. The revelation from *Wakantanka* had been similar for both young men, but only Swift Bear, Itazipe, and the *Wicasca Wakan,* Holy Man, knew what this was. Still the villagers learned that Charger and Kills And Comes had made a vow, as a result of their vision, to rescue white captives.

The Two Kettles thought that the young men had made a rash promise, for they still remained neutral in the Santee war with the whites and would not interfere with anything the Santee did. As the weeks went by, many forgot what the young men had vowed to do, but the villagers saw that where Charger led, Kills And Comes followed and Swift Bear was often with them.

Every day the three friends went to Primeau's store,

a temporary trading post the Frenchman had built above the abandoned Fort La Fromboise and old Fort Pierre. The place was still called Fort Pierre by some Indians and whites, but the Frenchman and his friends named the trading post Fort Primeau.

Primeau, understandably, encouraged Charger and Kills And Comes in their resolve to rescue white captives and promised to report any news that came his way. But when months passed and there was no word of Santee captives, Primeau and the young men began to think that perhaps the Santee would not venture so far to the west of their Minnesota home.

Still the young men went to Primeau's. Their visits were a welcome change from the monotony of the quiet Two Kettle village. So it was that on the morning of November seventeenth, as the three friends were lounging in the store, a runner came from the river bottom to announce the arrival of Major Galpin. The Major, his Yankton wife, and the miners followed close behind the excited young Indian runner. They came to rest a while and exchange news with Primeau before continuing their journey down the Missouri.

Galpin told Primeau of his party's encounter with the Santee band, which his Indian wife had correctly identified as hostile. "My woman really got suspicious," said Galpin, "when the Indians said they were peaceful hunters. She knew that the Sioux don't take old men hunting."

Major Galpin went on to tell of the ambush the Santee had set, their narrow escape, and most important to the listening Charger, of the white woman who had called for help from the shore.

"She was a ragged wretch," Galpin reported, "but before any of the Indians stopped her, she yelled that a Mrs. Duley, Mrs. Wright, and six white children were prisoners in the Santee camp."

Charger felt great joy. At last his vision could be fulfilled. "I will go to rescue the white captives!" he shouted joyfully. Kills And Comes and Swift Bear added their eager agreement.

Primeau laughed at the zealousness of the young men. "It will take more than just the three of you to rescue the prisoners. The Santee won't let the captives go easily. They'll put up a fight!"

"That's right," Major Galpin put in. "They seemed desperate to me. Undoubtedly, they've been hounded all the way from Minnesota. I wish we could stay to help you," he said to Charger. "I'd like to pay the savages back for giving us a scare, but we've got to be at Fort Randall in a few days."

"We will enlist others like ourselves to help us," Charger answered. "There are many Teton young men who long to do a brave deed. Come," he said to his friends, "we have much to do."

They made their plans as they rode back to the Two Kettle village. "The Santee are hungry," Charger said, urging his horse to a quicker pace. "So said Little Crow's man. We must gather our buffalo robes to trade to Primeau for food. We will hold a feast for the Santee so that they will meet with us."

"*Han*," agreed Kills And Comes, "and we must take good horses to trade for the captives, because the Santee like our strong, swift Teton mounts."

Charger kicked and whipped his horse into a gallop as they neared the village. "*Hoka Hey!*" the three shouted, riding furiously through the camp. The people scattered out of the way. Voices were raised in alarm and warriors ran for their weapons. At the far end of the camp circle, the young men jerked their horses into sharp, rearing turns. They sprinted back to the center, flaunting their skill on the wild-eyed animals. They ended the mad ride with a flourish as they reined their snorting, mouth-foamed horses to an abrupt halt.

Young men and giggling, excited maidens cheered their horsemanship. Older men and women scolded them for abusing the animals. The warriors denounced them for raising a false alarm.

"Brothers!" Charger shouted over the clamor as he, Kills And Comes, and Swift Bear danced their horses in tight circles, "the time has come to show your courage! Join us! We go to rescue white captives from the Santee."

"*Hoka Hey!*" whooped Kills And Comes. "We have had a vision!"

"*Hoka Hey!*" echoed Swift Bear. "We have made a vow!"

The people murmured in bewilderment at Charger's summons.

"*Wacintonsni,* fools!" called a warrior who turned his back and stomped disgustedly back to his tipi.

"*Wacinhnuni!* crazy!" another said, and now many of the people were moving away, muttering and shaking their heads at the rash boys. But here and there were young men who chafed at their inactivity and longed to prove their bravery.

"I will go," one cried. "And I," called out another; and another, until there were eight standing before Charger.

"*Ho!*" Charger exulted, calling the young men by name: "Sitting Bear, Four Bear, Pretty Bear, Mad Bear." He turned to his friend, saying "Swift Bear!

We will have the strength of *Mahto* on our mission!
Red Dog! Charging Dog! You bring the intelligence
of our friend *Shunka*. One Rib, Strikes Fire, Kills And
Comes, and Charger—all of us!" he shouted, sweeping
his hand over the eager young men. "We will be
soldiers against the Santee!"

"*Akicita wacintonsni*, Fool Soldiers!" one of the on-
lookers yelled scornfully.

Others picked up the name and soon many were
following after the young men laughing and chant-
ing, "Fool Soldiers, Fool Soldiers."

Charger ignored the derisive taunts and led the
young men to a secluded spot along the river where
they could make their plans.

"Do you have horses?" Charger asked his followers.

"*Han*, strong swift horses!"

"Are you willing to give up your horses in trade for
the captives?"

At Charger's question the young men were still and
looked at each other. Horses were the Teton's wealth
and hard to part with. But Kills And Comes and
Swift Bear shouted, "*Han*, gladly!" and the others
agreed.

"We are young," Charger began his harangue,
"none of us have counted *coup*. We have no knowledge of battle other than what our uncles and grand-

fathers have told us. Our journey to find the captives may be long and cold, for already the north wind has sent its snow warning.

"When we find the Santee we must be wily. Speak wisely and avoid bloodshed in which the captives might be harmed. But, if we must fight, we will do so bravely and be prepared to die!"

"*Han*! *Ho*!" shouted the young men. "We are not afraid to die!"

"You have heard," Charger went on, waving his hand toward the village, "what our people have called us. 'Crazy' and 'fools.' And," his voice lowered, "some will call us traitors because we dare to think of going to the aid of the whites.

"We will be ridiculed, perhaps even exiled, for what we plan to do. Are you strong enough to bear that?"

Again the young men shouted. "We are strong! We are not afraid!"

"*Waste*, good!" Charger was pleased. "Go now and prepare yourselves for the journey. Pack food and extra blankets. When all is ready gather at Primeau's, where I will be bartering buffalo robes for coffee and sugar." The young men scattered.

Primeau gave Charger full value and more for the robes, for the Frenchman knew it would be necessary that the band of young men hold an impressive feast for the Santee before any bargaining for the captives took place.

"After you rescue the captives," Primeau told Charger, "bring them to me. I will care for them until a way is found to take them to Fort Randall." He followed the youth out of the post to where the others were waiting. "Good luck!" he cried after the eleven young men who rode off, whooping and making their ponies prance down to the fording place on the river's bottom.

The young men, eager for adventure, swam their horses across the river and started north for the Santee camp. They rode steadily until twilight and then made camp for the night even though they were not tired. They wanted to keep the horses fresh, for they would be needed for barter as well as transportation on the return trip with the captives.

In the middle morning of the second day out of their village the Fool Soldiers, as they laughingly called themselves, came upon the camp of Bone Necklace, chief of a band of Yanktonais, on the Swan Lake Creek.

The Yanktonais made the young men welcome. Charger told them of his intent and inquired among Bone Necklace's people for news of the captives. Some of the Yankton warriors had come across the Santee band on a hunt.

"The Santee are led by White Lodge," the warriors said. "He has eighty lodges and is moving downstream to seek help from the Teton. There are many crying children in the Santee camp. They are hungry and destitute. This is why White Lodge attempted to capture the Galpin boat. He did not wish to kill them; he only wanted the boat's provisions."

Charger was pleased. "If the children in White Lodge's village are suffering, he will be desperate and ready to bargain. On!" he ordered his followers, "our mission will be easy!"

Optimistically, the Fool Soldiers rode about fifteen miles up the Missouri and found White Lodge's band setting up camp for the night. Near the Santee, but not among them, the Fool Soldiers pitched the one tipi they had brought for shelter.

Charger left his followers to prepare a feast of coffee, sugar, and hard bread, and he walked alone to invite the Santee to eat.

White Lodge greeted the young man in a cordial, yet reserved manner. He accepted Charger's invitation of food and soon Santee men led the way to the Fool Soldiers' camp. They drank the sweetened coffee which they had not had since leaving Shakotan. The women followed with cooking pots and other containers to carry the coffee in. They took back to the children the bits of bread and sugar the Fool Soldiers portioned out.

After White Lodge had eaten, Charger told the chief of his mission and requested a formal meeting with the Santee council.

"I do not bargain with boys," White Lodge declared scornfully.

"We have horses to trade," Charger said loudly and the Santee heard and pressed their chief to call the council.

Reluctantly White Lodge agreed and soon the council was seated around the warmth of the Fool Soldiers' fire. Charger produced a pipe, lit it with the proper ceremony, and passed it first, as a sign of honor, to White Lodge. After the pipe made its rounds of the council, the Fool Soldiers replenished the tin cups with coffee, and Charger spoke.

"Welcome, our cousins, the Santee," he greeted. "Our hearts are glad to see you in our land. We hold only good feelings for you."

"*Ho*," agreed the Santee and all of the young Fool Soldiers.

"You see us here," Charger said waving his hand to his followers and back to himself. "We are only young boys, as White Lodge has said. None of us have counted *coup* or seen battle. We know this. Our people call us crazy and fools. But we are brave in our hearts and want to do something good."

Charger paused, summoning the best words to impress the Santee. "If," he went on, "a man owns a thing he likes he will not part with it for nothing. We have come here to buy the white captives from you and give them back to their friends."

A murmur of astonishment at the young man's words went among the Santee and Charger quickly added, "We will give our own good horses for the captives. Our ponies are the best of the Two Kettle herd, the swiftest and strongest of all Teton horses. We will give *all* of our horses for the captives."

Again a murmur from the Santee, but this time it was a favorable sound. Charger pressed on. "Our offer to trade all of our horses proves that we want the captives very much. Our hearts are good and we want to do a good thing!"

Charger sat and stared into the fire. His heart was beating rapidly and his hands were wet with the sweat of relief now that he had spoken. But what would the Santee do? He dared not show disrespect and look at White Lodge, who sat in an ominous silence.

The chief slowly drank his coffee and ignored the arguments of his men. The young Fool Soldiers tried to sit stolidly serious, as befitted the moment. They knew that any impatient movement would be detrimental to their cause. White Lodge rose.

He arranged his blanket in dignified folds about his old body and stood, a stately, awesome figure, silhouetted against the fire. "We come from the east," the old chief began, "where the sky is red from the fires which burn the homes of whites who built on Santee land. The ground is red with the blood of whites the Santee have killed. The captives we have taken after the killing of many people. We can never again be friends with the whites for we have done many things which they think are bad.

"But we say," he shouted angrily, "that we have not done as much bad as the whites have done to us!

"We will not give up the captives!" White Lodge declared fiercely. "We will keep on doing what the whites say is a bad thing. We will fight until we are dead!"

The old chief sat and his council spoke loudly among themselves, some agreeing and others disagreeing with his words, but none rose. Charger motioned for Kills And Comes to speak.

"Our horses are the fastest of all the Tetons," Kills

And Comes bragged. "We will trade them for the white captives and they will carry you speedily and safely into battle."

The Fool Soldiers nodded in assent as Kills And Comes sat, and there was talk among the Santee. Charger waited for another of White Lodge's men to speak aloud, and when none rose he motioned to Swift Bear.

"Our horses are the strongest of all of the Tetons," Swift Bear cried. They will carry you far without tiring. We offer them in exchange for the captives."

White Lodge rose to still the loud argument among his council. "No!" he shouted. "We will not give up the captives!"

In the silence that followed Charger rose and spoke grimly. "White Lodge, you talk bravely. But you kill white men who have no guns. You steal women and children and run away to safety among the Teton where there are no soldiers. If you are brave, why did you not stay in Minnesota and fight the soldiers who had guns?" No one spoke after this accusing insult, but the Fool Soldiers held tightly to their weapons.

"Three times," Charger went on, "we have offered our horses for the captives. You have refused. Now," he said taking a step toward the Santee camp, "we will take the captives. We will put them on our horses and take them home!" He glared about the council.

"If you make trouble for us the soldiers with many guns will come against you from the east," he shouted and pointed. "And the Teton will come against you from the west," he pointed across the river. "Then we shall see if you are brave!"

The Fool Soldiers jumped to their feet, menacingly brandishing their guns and whooping war cries. The older Santee rose more slowly and began to back toward their camp and the protection of their warriors who waited in the background.

Before they could move far, a voice rose out of the darkness from the group of young Santee who did not sit in council. "Black Hawk," the voice cried to the eldest son of White Lodge who was in the council, "Why do you not speak? Why are you still?"

The elders turned and looked at the son of their chief. He hesitated and then stepped in front of White Lodge.

"Father," he addressed the chief, "I have love and respect for you and the others who are old, but," and he turned to the Fool Soldiers, "I also have respect for these young men who have shown great courage in daring to speak in such a manner to us.

"You have done right," Black Hawk said to Charger. "We have eaten your food and it was good. You are straight, brave young men, respected among your own people or they would not have let you come.

I know you, but my father does not know you." He paused and turned sad eyes upon White Lodge.

"My father, we are starving. We need the strong, swift horses of the Teton so that we may hunt far. We need the brave horses of the Teton to go to Little Crow in Canada, for we can never return to Minnesota. I have one white child in my lodge which I will give up even though my wife will grieve." He turned to face the other Santee. "Let you do as I have done and give up the captives!"

The Santee council huddled in conference. Their younger men shouted agreement with Black Hawk, for they wanted the Teton horses. White Lodge turned and headed back to the Santee camp; the council followed. Black Hawk came to Charger.

"We will exchange the captives for the horses," the chief's son said. "Wait here while we prepare the white women and children. We will have to convince the women who have adopted the three little girls to give them up. The white girls replaced Santee children who died and it will be like death again in the lodges of the mothers. We will send word when we are ready." Black Hawk walked away.

The Fool Soldiers took down their tipi and prepared to move quickly with the captives as soon as the exchange was made.

It was late at night when they were ready. The sky was black with low snow clouds that covered the night lights of the heavens. The Fool Soldiers huddled around their dying fire, blankets tightly wrapped against the chill wind that howled across the river. They waited. Gradually most of the young men curled up to sleep on the cold ground. Charger and Kills And Comes watched.

Charger was worried. "They are so long. Something must have gone wrong in the Santee camp."

"White Lodge has probably changed his mind again," Kills And Comes said. "But do not worry. The warriors want our horses. They will force the old man to trade."

The night was turning to a grayness that preceded dawn when the Fool Soldiers were summoned.

Charger woke his young men, and they caught the horses which had been hobbled nearby. They followed the Santee messenger to a large tipi which had been erected in the center of the camp. Here was where the exchange would be made. The Fool Soldiers tethered the horses near the entrance, and Strikes Fire stayed outside to watch the animals lest the desperate Santee steal them. The rest of the young men entered the tipi with Charger.

A fire burned in the center of the lodge. Black

Hawk, who sat across from the entrance, motioned for the Fool Soldiers to seat themselves on his left. On the other side of the tipi they saw one white woman with six children huddled about her.

Pity filled Charger's heart as he looked at the captives. The whites were poorly clothed, almost naked except for ragged cotton garments. Charger was struck by the vacant stare of the woman. She seemed unaware of her surroundings and made no effort to comfort the whimpering younger children. Two girls were at her sides, supporting her. One of them, the oldest of the children, bent to murmur to the little boy who snuggled closer to her. Charger saw that this girl could only bend one arm as she comforted the boy. She shushed the frightened wails of the other children and then proudly lifted her head and stared curiously at Charger and his followers. Charger was pleased that the girl was not afraid.

Black Hawk was speaking. "This is the woman Doo—Lee, and the two girls at her side are hers. The woman is mad," he said in disgust. "The other three girls have no mother. They were adopted by our women." His gaze moved to a grief-stricken Santee woman, her face blackened and her hair hanging in ragged strands over her face. Black Hawk's face softened with pity and Charger guessed that the woman was his wife, but the chief's son went on.

"The boy belongs to the other white woman, Wright, and lived in the lodge of my father."

"Where is the Wright woman?" Charger asked.

Black Hawk shook his head. "My father changed his mind about parting with her, but will let the boy go for one horse and a blanket."

Charger was dismayed. He knew now that the Santee had changed their minds about a wholesale exchange of captives for the horses. He would have to bargain for each captive individually.

Wearily he nodded and Black Hawk motioned for his wife to bring the Wright boy. The child was almost asleep, leaning against the girl who held him with her good arm. She gave the boy a little shake as the Indian woman approached. The boy cowered against the girl and Charger heard him cry, "Mama?" The girl bent her head and whispered encouragingly. The boy looked questioningly at her, and when she nodded with a smile he got up and let the woman lead him to Charger.

Charger handed her a blanket and gently took the small boy's hand. "*Hau, hoksila,*" he greeted and then realized that he should have spoken English. But, to his surprise, the child responded gravely, "*Hau, Waanatan.*"

Charger looked at Black Hawk, who was smiling. "The boy has been treated as a son in my father's lodge. He knows the language and manners of a Dakota boy and has been told your name."

The boy sat quietly beside Kills And Comes as Charger continued the bargaining. On and on he bartered through the day. Each captive, starting with the youngest child, went for a horse and blanket, or coffee and sugar. Finally, the oldest girl moved to the Fool Soldiers' side and when her mother was traded she spoke to Charger in halting Dakota.

"Waanatan, my mother is lame and will need my help to walk across the tipi."

Charger looked at the girl who seemed so much older than the twelve winters he had been told she was. "Can not the Santee woman help her?" he asked, afraid that if Sarah was allowed on the other side the Santee might not let her return.

Black Hawk spoke, "My woman does not want to touch the mad woman. Let the girl help her mother."

Charger understood the Santee aversion to madness, but he was still reluctant to let the girl go. "What is your name?" he asked the girl as he tried to think what to do.

"Sarah Duley," she answered. "But the Santee have called me Shining Hair."

Charger nodded. The Santee had named her well even though the fair hair was now grease-darkened and filthy. "Can not your mother walk alone?" he asked.

Sarah shook her head. "No. They have taken her crutch away." Her eyes filled with tears as she added, "And she must be led because she—she—," the girl faltered and looked away so that Charger would not see her weep.

Charger was overwhelmed with pity for the girl, sensing that she must have suffered terribly during captivity and that the mother had been an additional burden. "Go," he said to her.

Sarah moved to Martha's side and with her good arm touched the woman gently on the shoulder as if, Charger thought, the girl were the mother and the mother were the child. Martha looked up at her daughter with a wan smile and with the girl's help struggled to her feet. Charger saw that she was badly crippled as she limped across the tipi, leaning heavily on Sarah. Inwardly, he groaned. It would be difficult traveling with the maimed captive. He should have tried to strike a better bargain for the handicapped woman. All the Fool Soldiers had left was one horse and four guns and Mrs. Wright still had not been seen.

White Lodge entered the tipi carrying his war club and looked with disgust at the young Tetons. "Go," he commanded. "You have the captives!"

But Charger did not move. "There is still the Wright woman."

"No," White Lodge growled. "She is my wife. I am old; my first wife is old; my second woman is big with child. I need the white squaw in my lodge. She takes good care of me. I will not let her go!"

The Fool Soldiers exclaimed angrily and demanded that the chief release the white woman. Charger jumped to his feet. He was furious. "The Santee are liars!" he shouted. "They promised to exchange all of the captives for the horses. Instead they have taken much more. We will be hard-pressed with what we have left to get the captives safely to Primeau's post. Now White Lodge breaks his word even more by denying us the last captive. You are a treacherous people! You cannot be trusted by your cousins, the Teton!"

White Lodge rushed toward the captives, his war club raised. "I will kill them all!" he stormed. "I will kill all of you!"

The children screamed and clung to Sarah who glared at the threatening old man. The Fool Soldiers jumped in front of the captives to ward off White Lodge's swinging club. Black Hawk moved swiftly and caught his father's arm before the club struck.

"No!" Black Hawk yelled, and other Santee men

who had sat in on the exchange moved to restrain the furious chief.

"Black Hawk is wise!" Charger shouted above the uproar of crying children and yelling Santee.

The chief was forcibly seated by Black Hawk. The old man breathed heavily and glared at Charger. But before he could speak Sarah spoke in a soft voice.

"White Lodge has been good to us. We have been his children. Why does he wish to murder us now?"

Charger was amazed at the girl's poise. Her gentle voice stilled his angry words, and he spoke quietly as he saw that the angry chief had been calmed by the child's manner.

"The Santee forget," Charger spoke firmly, "that if you harm the captives, soldiers with many guns will give you no rest. They will pursue until you are all dead. Remember, too, that the Teton will also come against you."

Charger's heart pounded after he had spoken. He held his breath while he waited to see if the Santee believed him, for he knew that his threat was meaningless. It would be a long time before soldiers heard of the captives and the Santee could easily escape into the prairie wilderness. Nor could Charger count on the Teton coming to his aid. Yet, the destitute Santee did not know Charger was bluffing.

The Santee gathered around White Lodge. He listened to their arguments and at last, in sullen silence, nodded. Black Hawk signaled to his wife; she ran from the tipi to get the Wright woman.

"I will take a horse, a gun, and two blankets for the woman," White Lodge bargained.

"No!" Charger answered shortly. "We will give you one horse and two blankets. No more!"

White Lodge moved to rise, but was restrained by Black Hawk. Reluctantly the old man agreed to the counter offer.

Charger stood and motioned to his followers to take the woman and children out. Sarah understood the need to get away from the Santee as quickly as possible and urged the children to go with the Fool Soldiers while she grasped her mother's arm and led her after the others.

Charger waited alone until Julia Wright was brought into the tipi. Again his heart was filled with pity as he saw the woman's face. It was still bruised and swollen from White Lodge's anger of four days before when she had alerted Galpin of the captives presence in the Santee camp. She stared uncomprehendingly at Charger when he took her arm to guide her out of the tipi. "Come," he said in English, "you are free."

"Ohh," Julia sighed and then looked to where the old chief stood sadly staring at her. She moved to him impulsively and gently touched his arm. "Thank you," she said and then hurried after Charger.

White Lodge stood as if he had been struck.

Outside, Charger held to the woman's arm as he followed the Fool Soldiers who were carrying the younger children and hurrying the others forward. It was evening time again. They had been in the Santee camp for twenty-four hours and had had nothing to eat since they had feasted the Santee. Charger and Kills And Comes were weary from lack of sleep, but the party had to get as far away from the village as they could before night fell.

They were only a short distance from the Santee camp when Charger knew they had to stop. The wind that had been threatening snow for the past two days at last brought a November blizzard.

The small tipi was set up and everyone, except one of the Fool Soldiers who would stand guard, crowded in. The three blankets that remained were given to the captives, who fell immediately into exhausted sleep.

Charger was worried. He expected White Lodge to follow and try to retrieve the captives. The Fool Soldiers had only four guns for protection. All of the horses were gone and they had no food. They were more than one hundred miles from Primeau's post and the Two Kettle village. Would he be able to get the captives safely there? Charger wondered before he fell into a fitful rest.

It was still dark when One Rib, who had relieved the first guard, woke Charger. He roused the others and in minutes the party was moving down along the river banks through cold, swirling snow. Charger noticed that the Wright woman walked slower and slower until she was some distance behind. The girl, Sarah, had been following her mother, who was supported by Swift Bear. Now, Sarah turned and waited for Julia.

Charger waited until the woman and the girl came up to him. "You must keep up," he said to Julia, who nodded mutely.

"She has no shoes," Sarah told him, knowing that Julia would not say why she moved so slowly.

In his eagerness to get away from the Santee, Charger had not noticed the white woman's lack of footgear. He called for a brief rest and apologized to Julia. "I am sorry that I did not see your bare feet," he said sitting in the snow and removing his moccasins. "You must have covering for your feet or they will freeze."

"I have walked barefoot for a long time," Julia said.

She looked unbelievingly at him as he handed her his moccasins.

"But not in cold snow," Charger said urging the moccasins on her. "Put them on."

"But what will you wear?" Julia protested.

Charger smiled. "I will wrap strips of blanket around my feet." He ripped the cloth as he spoke. "Do not worry. A Teton's feet are tough like leather."

"How can I ever thank you?" Julia said as she tied the moccasins. "Not only for the moccasins, but for rescuing us. I was afraid White Lodge would kill us all. He was so angry after I called to the people in the boat. I had given up all hope of ever being released from captivity."

"It was the people in the boat who told us how to find you," Charger explained. He stood and motioned the party on.

Sarah took Nancy's hand and walked beside Charger. He soon saw that the little girl was having difficulty keeping up with his long strides. He stopped and lifted Nancy to his back. Sarah helped him wrap what was left of his blanket around her sister. Nancy was shivering with the cold and clung without protest to Charger's neck. The other small children were carried in the same way by the rest of the Fool Soldiers.

"Your little sister is no burden," Charger said.

"We have not had much to eat for a long time," Sarah said. "All of us, even the Santee, have been starving."

"Aah," Charger sighed, "poor little ones."

"I'm not so little," Sarah protested as she walked shoulder high with the young Teton. "I'm almost thirteen. How old are you?"

Charger smiled at the girl who seemed so much older than her years. "I have seen nineteen winters," he answered.

"How old are the others?"

"Pretty Bear is in his fifteenth winter. The others are between his age and mine."

"Aren't you all young to be doing a man's—" Sarah broke off not wanting to insult Charger. "I mean, among the Santee all of their warriors were old."

"The Teton become men at an early age," Charger answered. "And they must show their courage by doing a man's brave deed."

"Is that why you came to rescue us?"

Charger nodded. "That was part of it. We had heard of the Santee war long moons ago. We had sadness in our hearts at the bad things the Santee did to white women and children. I vowed to rescue white captives if ever I had the chance."

Sarah was amazed by this Indian. "How did you

learn to speak English so well?" she asked, for although she could converse with him in Dakota, he always spoke English to her.

"I visited with every white man who came on the river," Charger said. "I learned your language easily and even know some French from Primeau, the trader whose store is near my village. My people, the Two Kettle, say that I learned English and understand the white people because I am part white." He looked at Sarah to see if she believed him. "My grandfather was one of the first Americans to visit us."

"Who was that?" Sarah asked.

"He was called Lewis."

"Do you mean the explorer?"

"Do you know of him?"

"Yes," Sarah nodded. She did not know what to say to his claim which seemed to be important to him. She trudged along quietly for a while. Then she asked, "Do all of your people feel kindness towards white people?"

"No," Charger sadly shook his head. "Many of my people call me and my followers crazy and even traitors for going to the rescue of whites. We are known as the 'Fool Soldiers,' but we are not ashamed of the name. Is it foolish to do a good thing?"

Before Sarah answered, Four Bear, who had been

scouting ahead, came running to Charger. "There are three Yanktonais of the Bone Necklace village ahead of us. They say they have come to help us rescue the captives."

The Yanktonais had been breaking camp when Four Bear discovered them. They were Fast Walker, Don't Know How, and Walking Crane. The rescue party stopped and greeted them.

Walking Crane offered his horse to help the captives. A travois of tipi poles, which Red Dog had been dragging, was rigged and the smallest children placed upon it. Martha Duley rode on the horse.

Swift Bear, who had been guarding the rear, gave a warning call—White Lodge and a small war party were approaching on foot. Charger ordered his band to move.

"Go as fast as you can!" he shouted. "We will not stop to parley with the Santee this time. Swift Bear, if White Lodge fires, kill him!"

White Lodge did not shoot and followed only a little way after the Fool Soldiers. His bones ached from the long walk. The younger Santee warriors with horses no longer wanted captives in their camp and had refused to come with him. The men with him had come mainly to protect their chief, and even now were dissuading him from going on. Finally, the old man resigned himself to the loss of the captives and turned back upriver.

The Fool Soldiers gave a triumphant cheer as they watched the retreating White Lodge. Julia Wright sighed in relief and yet felt pity as she saw the chief stumble through the drifting snow, his head down in bitter defeat. "Poor old man," she whispered.

Charger heard her. "Do you feel sorrow for your enemy?" he asked in surprise.

Julia fell into step beside him. "Yes," she answered, smiling at his astonishment. "White Lodge was kind to me in his way, except toward the last. He kept his wives from beating me and my boy. He permitted Martha Duley to stay with us even though her injury slowed down the march.

"You have no hate in your heart?" Charger could not believe that this woman who had been so abused could feel charity.

Again Julia smiled and shook her head.

"And you?" he asked Sarah.

"No."

"But your mother has suffered more than any of you," Charger said pointing to the crippled woman on the horse.

"I know," Sarah said sadly. "My mother has never been very strong, nor able to bear much pain or distress. But the Santee treated us children as if we were their own. The old woman, Anna, who lived with us in her son's tipi, cared for Nancy and me as if we were her own grandchildren. She dressed mother's wound and mine—she—" Sarah's voice broke and her eyes brightened with tears, "loved Nancy and me. When she knew that we were going to leave with you, she cut her hair, blackened her face and mourned as if we had died."

Charger's heart was stirred by the girl's compassion for her captors. He knew that her feelings for Indians were unacceptable to most white people. He thought she would be considered as foolish by her people as he was by the Two Kettles. Charger felt a bond between himself and the white girl.

The rescue party reached the Bone Necklace camp on the evening of November twenty-first. Charger gratefully accepted the Yanktonais' offer to spend the night. He and his friends were weary after the twenty-four hour parley with the Santee, and the weakened captives were exhausted.

The Yanktonais gave the captives food and blankets. Charger slept well that night, knowing that the Yanktonais watched over them. The next morning Bone Necklace gave the Fool Soldiers an old cart he had found along the river. All of the children could ride now, and the group could move faster. The chief also gave them extra blankets and enough food to last until they reached Primeau's post.

Martha could not ride on the horse because of the cart's shafts lashed to its sides, and when she was placed in the cart with the children, the load was too heavy for the animal. So Charger divided his young men into three groups to spell each other in pushing the cart to aid the horse. He and Kills And Comes were the only ones in the last group, and Julia insisted on helping them.

The snow had stopped, but they made a long, cold march before Charger called a halt. They camped that night along the river in the spot which the whites called Forest City because of the thick grove of trees which gave shelter from the harsh wind. It was a good camp. There was fuel for the night fire, and the captives slept under the Yanktonais blankets. The Fool Soldiers slept huddled close together, warmed by their body heat.

As the weak sun rose in the morning, so did the Fool Soldiers and the captives. The younger children cried fretfully when they had to leave the warm tipi and get in the open cart. All of them were coughing and had runny noses. Julia told Charger that the two Ireland girls were feverish. Charger knew he would have to get them to Primeau's soon.

He picked a route away from the Missouri and up

to the prairie where the traveling was easier, even if there was nothing to break the wind. The group cut across the oxbow of the river as night came on, but Charger did not permit more than a brief stop for eating and rest. He pushed the party on through the night, and at daybreak they were on the river bottom, and home was west across the Missouri.

The river widened at the fording place and was not as deep as it was up stream. But the shallow stream was covered with the first winter ice, and Charger knew the crossing would be difficult because of the current and the icy water. Kills And Come volunteered to go first to test the ice and find the best way. Charger watched anxiously as his brother-friend walked on the firm ice near the shore. A little way out, however, he plunged through the thinner film into shoulder-deep water. But Kills And Comes went on. On the opposite shore, as he came shivering out of the water, he was met by Primeau, who had watched daily for their return. With the Frenchman's assistance, he stumbled out onto the sandy shore.

The trader summoned his friends Dupree and La Plante from the post. They carried Primeau's sturdy boat into the water and poled across the river, following the trail Kills And Comes had broken through the ice.

The boat made several trips back and forth across the Missouri, and soon the captives and the Fool Soldiers were in the secure warmth of Primeau's post.

"You did it, Charger!" Primeau exulted as he bustled about preparing hot drink and food. "Poor children," the trader said with tears in his eyes as he surveyed the pitiful condition of the captives, "and poor mothers. That one . . ." he said sadly of Martha Duley and shook his head. "How long have you been in captivity?" he asked Julia.

"Since August," Julia answered as she gratefully sipped hot coffee. "But it has seemed forever."

Once they were warm, the Fool Soldiers became restless and longed to go to their homes. "I deliver the captives safely to you," Charger said to Primeau. The trader nodded and answered, "I will give them food and clothing. They will rest for a few days, and then Dupree and La Plante will take them to Fort Randall and the soldiers."

Julia went to Charger and shook his hand. "We will never forget what you have done for us."

Charger nodded and moved towards the door to follow his young men who had already left. Sarah Duley ran to him, grabbed his hand, and kissed it. "Thank you," she sobbed.

Charger jerked his hand away as if it were burned.

He looked down at the weeping white girl and his heart beat painfully fast, but he said nothing as he turned and walked away.

V

Mankato

"Have you heard anything of the Lake Shetek captives?" William J. Duley asked General Henry Sibley, the commander of the prison which held Santee prisoners in the village of Mankato.

The General had been harried by vengeful settlers demanding the immediate execution of 260 Indians who had been convicted of the worst crimes committed during the Minnesota Uprising. But he had been hindered by a Presidential order delaying the execution until Lincoln himself could review the evidence, and just the day before he had received another Presidential order that he knew would infuriate the settlers. Now he wearily answered William Duley.

"There has been no word, Mr. Duley. When I hear anything at all about the Shetek captives, I most certainly will inform you at once."

"I would appreciate that, General," Duley said. "I'm the only one left in Mankato."

"Have the other Shetek survivors left?"

"Yes," Duley nodded. "Mrs. Eastlick, her two boys, and Mrs. Hurd have been gone for two weeks now. Tom Ireland and John Wright left yesterday for Wisconsin. They gave up waiting for word. I'm to write them as soon as I hear anything."

General Sibley rose and walked around his desk to usher Duley out of his office. It was difficult for the commander to feign sympathy for the settler. He had seen and heard so much of the horrors of the Uprising—on both sides—that he had had to harden his heart to keep his sanity.

"Rest assured," he said to Duley, taking the man's arm, "you will have news of your captives as soon as I receive any."

"Not only of the captives, General," Duley said fiercely. "I want to know where that murdering White Lodge and his band of savages are. They killed my sons. I found their mutilated bodies after I regained consciousness. Mrs. Eastlick told me she saw

White Lodge carry off my wife and daughters—Lord knows what horrors they have experienced as captives! I want to see that White Lodge and his followers are given the justice they deserve for their fiendish acts!"

General Sibley stood quietly, staring at Duley, appalled by the settler's furious need for vengeance. Then a thought came to him that might solve one of his problems.

"Hmmn," he murmured, turning back to his desk. "I understand, Mr. Duley, and again I promise to assist you." He walked to the window which overlooked a busy scene of carpenters pounding together the huge gallows on which the convicted Indians would be hung.

"Perhaps, Mr. Duley, you can also be of assistance to me."

"What would that be, General?"

"On December 26th thirty-eight of the convicted Indians are scheduled to hang—"

"Only thirty-eight!" the settler interrupted harshly. "But there were two hundred and sixty of the murderers convicted! What's going to happen to the rest?"

General Sibley picked up from his desk the order he had received the day before and looked at it as he spoke. "President Lincoln pardoned them. There were forty condemned to die as a token punishment, but one of them has already died and the other has had his sentence commuted to life imprisonment."

Duley angrily slammed his fist against the back of a chair, sending it skidding across the room. The General resented the settler's action but said nothing.

"As I said," Sibley continued, the hanging is scheduled for the day after Christmas. I cannot find a hangman."

William Duley stared at Sibley, at first not comprehending the commander's meaning. Then he smiled. "Are you asking me to cut the trip rope?"

Sibley nodded. "You will be paid five twenty-dollar gold pieces for the job."

"No money needed," Duley said grimly. "I'll do it for nothing. One hundred times that amount wouldn't be enough for the pleasure it will give me to send those red devils to hell!"

Christmas was past and William Duley stood waiting at the scaffold. He had been there since dawn, when the thirty-eight condemned Indians began their death songs within the stone walls of the prison. At ten o'clock, the Santee men were marched from the prison; their wrists were bound and white muslin hoods covered their faces. They marched silently as hundreds of curious white men, women, and even children watched from the streets, windows, and roof tops. Weeping Indian women, wives and mothers of the condemned men, followed but were held back by soldiers.

As the Indians mounted the big platform of the gallows, they began again their Dakota death chant. Guards led them to places under dangling nooses, ten on each side and nine each on the ends. Fourteen-hundred and nineteen soldiers moved into an impenetrable formation around the scaffold.

The Presbyterian missionary, Stephen Riggs, who had devoted his life to serving the Santee, stood below and prayed aloud for the souls of the condemned.

The drummers began a slow, measured beat, and the Indians on the platform began stepping in a last dance. Their voices, muffled by the hoods, rose as they swayed and stamped their feet to the drum beat. Some shouted their names and the names of their comrades, and despite their bound wrists others moved to their neighbors and clasped hands in farewell. The platform rocked and swayed dangerously as the dance became more violent. Officers shouted to the guards to stop the dancing and singing. The soldiers secured the nooses over the Indians' heads and the dancing stopped, but the song of death went on.

William Duley found himself dripping with a nervous sweat as the drummers began the second drum roll. He wiped his trembling hands on his trousers and tightly grasped a sharp knife. The third roll of the drums, his signal, started and he stepped forward. His hand steadied and with a dreadful shout he cut the trip rope.

The platform dropped and the death song was stilled.

GLOSSARY

Akicita (*ah-ķee-chi-tah*): soldier

Coup (*coo*): from the French, meaning to strike. The act of coup was to strike or touch an enemy without killing or being killed and was one of the bravest things a Sioux warrior could ever do.

Dakota or Lakota (*dah-ķo-tah, lah-ķo-tah*): what the Sioux called themselves, meaning friendly people.

Eyapaha (*á-yah-pah-ha*): word carrier

Han or Ho (*hanh, ho*): an expression of agreement, yes

Hau (*how*): a greeting

Hinh (*heenh*): an exclamation of shock, fear, sadness

Hiya (*hee-yah*): no

Hiyohi (*hee-yo-hee*): come

Hoka Hey (*ho-ķah-hey*): a battle cry

Hokśila (*hoķ-shee-la*): boy

Itazipe (*ee-tah-zee-peh*): bow

Kunśi (*ķoo-shee*): grandmother

Mahto (*mah-toh*): bear

Minnishoshay (*min-nee-sho-shay*): the Teton name for the Missouri River

MINNESOTA (*min-nee-soh-tah*): smoky water

MOON WHEN ALL THINGS RIPEN: the Teton name for the month of August

MOON WHEN DEAD LEAVES ARE SNAPPING AND SHAKEN OFF BY THE WIND: the Santee name for the month of September

MOON WHEN THE DEER LOST THEIR HORNS: the Santee name for the month of October

MOON WHEN WINTER SETS IN: the Teton name for the month of November

SANTEE (*sahn-tee*): knife, one of the three main divisions of the Sioux

SHUNKA (*shoon-kah*): dog

SIOUX (*soo*): the French name for the Dakota Indians

TAOYA TE DUTA (*tah-oh-ya teh doo-tah*): His Red People, the name of a Santee chief also known as Little Crow

TETON (*tee-tahn*): Dwellers on the Plains, one of the three main divisions of the Sioux

TIPSINA (*tip-see-nah*): wild turnip

UPO (*oo-po*): an expression to command attention

WAANATAN (*wah-nah-tahn*): one who charges, or the charger

WACINHNUNI (*wah-chin-hnu-nee*): crazy

WACINTONŚNI (*wah-chin-tohn-shnee*): the Teton word for fool

WAKAN (*wah-kahn*): holy, mysterious

WAKANTANKA (*wah-kahn-tahn-kah*): the Great Spirit, the Sioux name for God

WAKEYESKA (*wah-keh-yeh-ska*): White Lodge, the name of a Santee chief

WASTE (*wash-tay*): good

WICAŚCA WAKAN (*wee-cha-sha wah-kahn*): Holy Man

WITKOKOKA (*wee-ko-ko-kah*): the Santee word for fool

YANKTON (*yank-ton*): Campers at the End, one of the three main divisions of the Sioux

YANKTONAIS (*yank-ton-nays*): Little Yankton, a sub-tribe 'of the Yankton